"I waited ... wait one hour longer."

"I can't come over to your hotel at this time of night," Jessica gasped.

"Why not?" His deep, dark voice thickened audibly. "You won't be going home again...."

Jessica was shattered. *Now...tonight?*

"And if you don't come tonight, the deal's off."

"That's totally unreasonable!"

"But what I want," Carlo asserted.

"You can't always have what you want—"

"Can't I?" He laughed softly and the phone went dead.

LYNNE GRAHAM was born in Northern Ireland and has been a keen Mills & Boon reader since her teens. She is very happily married with an understanding husband, who has learned to cook since she started to write! Her three children keep her on her toes. She has a very large Old English sheepdog, who knocks everything over, and two cats. When time allows, Lynne is a keen gardener.

Books by Lynne Graham

Don't miss any of our special offers. Write to us at the following address for information on our newest releases.

Harlequin Reader Service
U.S.: 3010 Walden Ave., P.O. Box 1325, Buffalo, NY 14269
Canadian: P.O. Box 609, Fort Erie, Ont. L2A 5X3

LYNNE GRAHAM

The Heat of Passion

Harlequin Books

TORONTO • NEW YORK • LONDON
AMSTERDAM • PARIS • SYDNEY • HAMBURG
STOCKHOLM • ATHENS • TOKYO • MILAN
MADRID • WARSAW • BUDAPEST • AUCKLAND

ISBN 0-373-11908-9

THE HEAT OF PASSION

First North American Publication 1997.

CHAPTER ONE

EBONY-BLACK hair against a crisp linen pillow, brown skin against a blindingly white sheet, and tiger's eyes burning with blatant cruelty and triumph into hers. In horrified rejection of the imagery that had sprung into her mind, Jessica shuddered violently, dimly aware that she was still in the grip of severe shock.

Abruptly, she was dredged from her turmoil by the insistent shrill of the telephone in the hall. Reluctantly she answered the summons, carefully shutting the lounge door behind her so that her father was not disturbed.

'Jessica . . . ?'

She froze, her stunningly beautiful face white as snow between the silken wings of her silver-blonde hair. Her breath caught in her throat in a strangled gasp. The receiver dropped from her nerveless fingers and swung towards the floor.

That voice, that truly unforgettable voice...deep, dark and rich as golden honey. He said her name as no one else had ever said it. She hadn't heard him speak in six long years and yet recognition was instantaneous and terrifying. Her throat closing over, she bent down to retrieve the phone.

'I am so sorry to have startled you,' Carlo Saracini purred, lying between his even white teeth.

Her own teeth clenched. She wanted to reach down the telephone line and slap him stupid. And feeling that way again...feeling that alien surge of raw violent hatred which he alone invoked...scared her rigid. Her mouth went dry. 'What do you want?'

5

'I'm in a very generous mood,' he imparted with a husky edge to his slow slightly accented drawl. 'I'm prepared to offer you a meeting——'

Her fingers clenched like talons round the receiver. 'A meeting...why?'

'Can it be that you haven't seen your father yet?' he murmured.

She went white. 'I've seen him,' she whispered, not troubling to add that Gerald Amory was still in the room next door.

'Embezzlement is a very serious offence.'

'He had gambling debts,' Jessica protested in a feverish undertone. 'He panicked...he didn't mean to take the money from the firm! He was borrowing it——'

'Euphemistically speaking,' Carlo inserted with more than an edge of mockery.

'Amory's used to belong to him,' Jessica reminded him with helpless bitterness.

'But it doesn't now,' Carlo traded softly. 'Now it belongs to me.'

Jessica's teeth gritted. Six years ago, burdened by the demands of a wife with expensive tastes, ageing machinery and falling profits, Gerald Amory had allowed Carlo to buy the family firm. Duly reinstalled as chief executive, her father had seemed content and, with new equipment and unparalleled export opportunities through the parent conglomerate, Amory Engineering had thrived.

Guilt stabbed like a knife into Jessica. If it had not been for her, Carlo Saracini would never have come into their lives. If it had not been for her the firm would still have belonged to her father. If it had not been for her, Gerald Amory would not now be facing criminal charges for embezzlement. Nausea stirred in her stomach, churned up by a current of raw loathing so powerful, she could taste it.

'Dad intended to repay the money...if it hadn't have been for the audit, you wouldn't even have found out!' she said in desperation.

'Why do you think I spring occasional surprise audits on my companies?' Carlo enquired gently. 'Employees like your father get greedy and sometimes they get caught as he has with their hands trapped in the till.'

Jessica trembled, her heartbeat thundering deafeningly in her eardrums. His deliberate cruelty appalled her. 'He wasn't greedy...he was desperate!'

'I'm willing to meet you tonight. I'm staying at the Deangate Hall. I'm sure I don't need to tell you which suite I'll be occupying. Eight,' he specified. 'I will wait one minute past the hour, no more. If you're not there, there'll be no second chance, *cara*.'

Aghast at the site he had specified and absolutely enraged by his instinctive sadism, Jessica gasped, 'Don't waste your time! I'll see you in hell before I set foot inside that hotel again!'

'You must have been quite a sight limping out on one shoe that afternoon,' Carlo mused provocatively. 'The chambermaid found the other one under the bed. I still have it. Cinderella's slipper——'

'How dare you?' she seethed down the phone in outrage.

'And as I recall it, you damned near left something far more intimate behind,' Carlo breathed reflectively.

Scarlet to her hairline, Jessica slammed down the receiver before she could be further reminded of her own appalling, inexcusable weakness that day. No, the very last thing she wanted to think about right now was that day at the Deangate, six years ago.

No more, she wanted to scream, no more. But of course, she wouldn't. Jessica didn't scream. Jessica hated to lose control. She had grown up sobbing silently behind closed doors, covering her ears from the sound of her mother screaming at her poor father. And she had sworn then that she would be different and that her own fiery temper would be subdued by every means within her power. She would be strong without passion. And if she stayed away from the passion, she would not be hurt.

The worst thing of all now had to be looking back, seeing how she had broken her own rules and how she had suffered accordingly. Struggling to escape those frightening echoes from the past, Jessica returned to her father.

Grey with strain, he glanced up and began talking again, not even acknowledging that she had been out of the room, so cocooned in his own problems that he might as well have been on another planet.

'I had to hand over all my keys...even my car keys. I wasn't allowed to enter my own office again,' Gerald Amory relived painfully. 'Then I was escorted out of the building by two security guards...it was a nightmare!'

Those must have been Carlo's instructions. Hadn't her father deserved just a little bit more consideration? Couldn't he have been allowed to retain even a tiny sliver of dignity?

'Dad...' Her voice suspended by choking tears, Jessica darted across the room to offer comfort but her father pulled away from her.

'I would have treated a thief the same way——' The admission was stark.

'You're not a thief!'

But Gerald Amory made no response.

Every which way Jessica looked, she felt responsible. She should have been there for her father, should have seen that he was in trouble. A week after Carlo had bought Amory Engineering, Jessica's mother had walked out and started a divorce. The amount of cash from the sale had proved too severe a temptation for Carole Amory. Bad as the marriage had been, Gerald Amory had been utterly devastated. Her father had adored her mother. He had been terrifyingly loyal and forgiving through her every extra-marital affair. He would have done anything to keep her...he had crawled, begged, pleaded. The only person relieved by Carole's departure had been her daughter.

But she should have seen the immense vacuum that had opened up in her father's life. She had watched him turn into a workaholic, living and breathing business and profit because that was all he had left. Why hadn't it occurred to her that, as the firm thrived and made all the money her greedy mother could ever have wanted, her father must have bitterly resented the fact that the firm was no longer his and that those healthy profits had come too late to sustain his shaky marriage?

But gambling...?

'It was somewhere to go, something to do,' he proffered while she stared back at him aghast. 'And then I started losing and I thought I couldn't go on losing forever...'

The silence went on and on and then abruptly and without any warning, Gerald Amory rose heavily from his seat and moved with the shambling gait of a much older man towards the front door.

'Where are you going?' Jessica demanded, her violet eyes almost purple with the strength of her distress.

'Home...I need to be on my own, Jess...please understand that.'

In despair, she hurried down the path after him, 'Dad, we can cope better with this together! Please stay,' she pleaded.

'I'm sorry. Not now, Jess,' he breathed tightly, unable to look at her.

Cope with the shame, the publicity, the court case? With the loss of his home, his job, his self-respect? Would he be able to cope? It was a tall order, she registered dully, especially for a man of his age. But what alternative was there? You coped, you survived. If Jessica had learnt anything in recent years, it was that truth.

Yet struggle as she did she could no longer keep her mind fully focused on her father's problems. The past was surging back to her, the past she had buried six years ago...

The day she had met Carlo Saracini she had been in London, shopping for her trousseau in the company of a friend. It had been less than two months before her wedding to Simon. She hadn't been wearing her engagement ring. One of the stones had worked loose and it had been in the jeweller's for repair.

She had been standing chatting to Leah at a busy intersection, waiting on the lights changing so they could cross. Somebody behind her in the crowd had pushed her and she had fallen into the road, practically beneath the wheels of Carlo's chauffeur-driven limousine.

She didn't remember falling. She had knocked herself out. What she did remember was coming dizzily back to consciousness before the ambulance arrived and focusing on the most extraordinary golden eyes above hers. She had been suffering from concussion. As a child she had had a story-book about a tiger with eyes that were pools of brilliant gold. So, naturally she had stared. She had never before seen eyes that shade.

'Stay still...don't speak.' Carlo had been rapping out autocratic instructions in every direction, including hers.

'I'm fine——'

'Keep quiet,' she had been told.

'It's only my head and I want to get up...' She had begun trying to move.

A brown hand like a giant weight had forestalled such daring.

'Look...I want to get up,' she had said again, embarrassed eyes flickering over the gathering crowd of onlookers.

'You are not getting up...you could have injured your spine.'

Her temper had begun to spark. 'My spine is OK...I'm OK——'

'We will have a doctor tell us that.' He had continued to stare down at her with the most phenomenal intensity and then he had run a forefinger almost caressingly along her delicate jawbone. 'I shall never forgive myself for hurting something so incredibly beautiful...'

Leah had been totally useless, having hysterics somewhere in the background. Jessica had found herself in a private ambulance, accompanied not by her friend but by Carlo.

'She will follow in my car,' he had asserted, getting in the way of the paramedics while simultaneously telling them what to do.

She just hadn't had the strength to fight Carlo Saracini off that day. Her head had been aching fit to burst and her stomach churning with nausea. She had shut her eyes to escape, telling herself that this volatile and domineering foreigner was simply attempting to make amends for an accident which hadn't been his fault in the first place.

She had been taken to a clinic, subjected to an alarmingly thorough examination against her will and tucked into a bed in a very expensively decorated room.

'I want to go home,' she had protested to the nurse. 'This is so unnecessary.'

Carlo had strode through the door, splintering waves of vibrant physical energy that seemed to charge the very atmosphere and drive out all tranquility.

'Where's Leah?' she had whispered, shaken that he was still around.

'I had her taken home. She was too distressed to be of any assistance. I understand that your parents are abroad and will not be home until tomorrow. Do you wish me to contact them?'

'I don't even know your name,' she had begun through clenched teeth.

'Carlo Saracini,' he had murmured with a slashing and brilliant smile. 'How do you feel?'

'I just want to go home...don't you ever listen to anything people say?'

'Not if I don't want to hear it,' Carlo had admitted.

'Look, all this...' She had indicated the fancy room with embarrassment. 'It's not necessary. I fell into the road. Your car didn't touch me. It's not as if I'm going to sue you or anything, and all this fuss——'

'Is my wish,' he had inserted silkily, scanning her slender shape beneath the bedclothes with blatant appreciation, making her cheeks ignite into sudden colour and sweeping up to her face with yet another smile. 'I can't take my eyes off you. You may have noticed that. Then, you must be accustomed to a great deal of male attention.'

'Not since I got engaged,' she had muttered stiffly, infuriated by the fashion in which he was openly looking her over as if she were an object on a supermarket shelf there for the taking.

He had stilled, golden eyes narrowing and flaring. 'You belong to another man?'

'I belong to no man, Mr Saracini!' Jessica had snapped.

'You will belong to me,' he had murmured with utter conviction.

She had honestly thought he was nuts. Nobody had ever talked to her like that before. Mind you, she had been to Greece once on holiday and had noted that radical feminism had yet to find a foothold there. But that a male dressed with such apparent sophistication in a superbly tailored mohair and silk blend suit, a male who spoke with an air of culture and education, should make such primitive statements had astonished her.

'I'm getting married in six weeks,' she had informed him flatly, involuntarily studying his strikingly male features before she realised what she was doing and hurriedly looked away again.

'We'll see . . .' And Carlo had laughed indulgently, the way you laughed when a child said something innocently amusing.

Jessica sank back to the present and discovered that she was shivering. Her first thought was for her father. No matter what he said, he shouldn't be alone. Grabbing up a coat, she let herself out of the tiny cottage she rented and climbed into her car to drive over to his house.

'But your father's at work, Mrs Turner. What would he be doing home at this time of the day?' Her father's housekeeper studied her with a questioning frown.

Jessica swallowed hard, fighting to keep her face unconcerned. 'I thought he was finishing early.'

'Well, he didn't mention it to me.'

'I'll catch him later.' Jessica climbed back into her car.

Dear God, where had her father gone? She must have been out of her mind to let him wander off like that in the state he was in! Another little voice asked her what she was doing. Her father had said he needed time on his own. She was not his keeper. Shouldn't she respect his wishes? But the nagging sense of urgency nibbling at her nerve-endings wouldn't leave her alone.

Reluctantly she went home again. Carlo...she couldn't get Carlo out of her mind. Would she go to the Deangate Hall Hotel to crawl and beg and plead as once her father had done with her mother? Her stomach gave a sensitive heave. What would be the point? She *knew* Carlo Saracini. There was no way he would let her father off the hook. Carlo wanted revenge. He couldn't touch Jessica but he knew just how deep the bond was between father and daughter. It would be a sweeter revenge than any that dark Machiavellian intellect might have calculated.

'Some day you will come to me on your knees and beg me to take you... and I will break you.'

As she remembered, perspiration dampened her short upper lip.

Carlo Saracini had destroyed her life. He had hacked to pieces everything she held dear. Her love for Simon, her happiness, her tranquillity... and in the end her self-respect. She had fought him to the very last shred of her endurance and then had learnt the secret of her own frailty in a shattering hour of self-discovery. Shuddering with disgust, she shut out the memories but the humiliation and the shame lived on as strongly as ever.

Carlo was one hundred per cent predator. Ruthless, unforgiving, utterly intolerant of those weaker than himself. She would never ever forget the way he had looked at her on her wedding-day. With smouldering incredulous fury and naked hatred. The Alpha male, fabulously rich, indecently successful and stunningly handsome... rejected. Right up until the very last moment Carlo had expected her to change her mind and fling herself at his feet.

'I will never forgive you.'

Carlo Saracini's parting assurance outside the church door. She had been shaking so badly by that stage, Simon had practically been holding her upright. She looked like a ghost in the wedding photographs. Simon had assured her that he had forgiven her but as she lived day in, day out with the farce of her marriage, she had never been able to forgive herself.

Jessica raised an unsteady hand to her pounding temples, struggling with the greatest of difficulty to regain her concentration. Why on earth hadn't she realised before now that her father was in trouble? She had been too involved in her own problems, she acknowledged wretchedly.

Simon had been ill for a long time before his death. His business had crashed in the recession, leaving nothing but debts. Her father had urged her to come home but she had refused. She hadn't wanted to turn into the Daddy's little girl she had been before her marriage. She hadn't even had a job in those days. All she had ever thought about as a teenager was marrying Simon and having children. She shoved that particular recollection away with helpless bitterness.

Carlo had invited her to the Deangate to gloat over her father's downfall. A sadist to the backbone, he wanted to experience her pain personally. Why should she give him the satisfaction when she knew that he would not allow her father to go unpunished? No way was she going to keep that appointment at the Deangate Hotel!

Jessica climbed out of her car. It was dark and cold and wet, just like that other day long ago, that day she couldn't bear to remember. She straightened slight shoulders, tightened the sash on her serviceable beige raincoat and lifted her head high as she crossed the car park. *This* was for her father. *This* was her duty. So what if she felt physically sick at the prospect of seeing Carlo Saracini again? She owed this meeting to her father.

If the opportunity to watch her squirm gave Carlo a kick, maybe...just maybe it might be possible to persuade him to mitigate the severity of the punishment he was doubtless planning. Naturally the money would have to be repaid. And the only way that could be done would be by the sale of her father's home. And since houses didn't sell overnight, Carlo would have to be prepared to allow time for that sale to take place. All that she would ask would be that he did not drag her father through court and utterly destroy him.

Was that so much to ask? she wondered tautly as she approached the reception desk of the Deangate Hotel. Yes, it was a great deal to ask of a male of Carlo's ilk.

'Can I help you?' a smiling receptionist asked, jolting her out of her reverie.

'My name is Turner. I have an appointment with Mr Saracini at eight,' Jessica advanced with all the appearance of a job-hunter, mentioning an interview.

'I'll call up...Mrs Turner.' The young woman's eyes flicked over the wedding-ring on Jessica's hand.

Jessica moved away a step or two, a nervous hand brushing up to check the sleek severity of the French pleat she had employed to confine her eye-catching hair.

'I'm sorry, Mrs Turner...'

Jessica turned back. 'Is there a problem?'

'Mr Saracini...' The brunette cleared her throat awkwardly.

'Yes?' Jessica pressed tightly.

'He says that he does not recognise your name——'

'I beg your pardon?' Jessica breathed in deeply, hot pink abruptly washing her ivory pale complexion as she belatedly understood. Carlo had taken exception to her marital name. One slim hand braced on the edge of the desk. She swallowed hard on her fury. 'Try Amory,' she suggested thinly.

'Amory?' the receptionist repeated with a perplexed look.

'Just tell Mr Saracini that a Miss Amory is here,' Jessica enunciated between gritted teeth.

'You can go up,' she was told ten seconds later.

The lift disgorged two couples in full evening dress. She walked in, her heart in her throat. The Deangate Hotel was one of the most expensive country house establishments in Britain. It lay five miles out of Barton and few locals had the income required to avail themselves of such unashamed luxury. Jessica had always hated the place. This was where her mother had come

to meet men. This was where she had trysted with her
lovers. And there was a peculiar agony to Jessica's
awareness that it was in this very same establishment
that she had forever lost her claim to the moral high
ground.

Had she been smug and pious in those days? Her
mother had once accused her of that...

'You're just like your father,' Carole had condemned
with bitter resentment. 'You're so bloody virtuous, you
ought to be wearing a halo! So smug, you make me sick!
But you won't get through life like that. Some day you're
going to fall off your pedestal and fall flat on your pious
little face and it'll serve you damned well right!'

And she had fallen, boy, had she fallen. With an inner
shudder of distaste, Jessica stepped out of the lift, outraged by the direction of her thoughts. She had come
here without allowing herself to think of what she had
to face at journey's end but the eerie familiarity of her
surroundings was like a razor twisting inside her.

Six years ago, she had stalked along this corridor in
a rage to tackle Carlo Saracini. And even this length of
time after the event it was quite impossible for her to
explain how she had very nearly ended up in his bed.
The two of them... like animals, her clothing half off,
his hands on her body, her hands on his. Obscene, she
reflected with a stab of revulsion. And had it not been
for the noisy entrance of the chambermaid into the
lounge next door to the bedroom, that disgusting incident might have gone considerably further than it had.

Youth had given her an edge, she appreciated now.
Youth often knew no fear. That had been her strength
at the beginning. She really hadn't realised what she was
up against. Carlo Saracini, a shark in a sleepy back-
water. Superbly clever, insidiously calculating and terrifyingly dangerous. Fear might have protected her, but
she hadn't learnt to fear him until it was far too late.

But she was scared now, scared enough to please even the most merciless sadist. Not scared for herself... but for her father. An old-fashioned gentleman, who had grown up in a far different world from Carlo Saracini's.

She came to a halt in front of the door and briefly closed her eyes. Crawl, she told herself. That's what he wants. And if he gets what he wants, maybe destroying her father would seem less appealing. She knocked the door and braced herself. It was opened almost immediately by a young man.

'Come in, Miss Amory,' he said gravely.

The lounge of the suite was unchanged. Her fluttering gaze fell on an overstuffed lemon brocade sofa and helplessly she thought, It started there. Her skin burned.

She heard Carlo say something in Greek. The product of a marriage between an Italian and a Greek, Carlo was equally at home in either language. Her spine stiffened. He strolled into view and the door slid softly shut behind her.

Jessica couldn't take her eyes off him. He repelled her. Every earthy, oversexed inch of him absolutely repelled her and there was a certain deadly attraction to that amount of revulsion, she told herself. He moved with the grace of a prowling tiger. He had the face of a dark fallen angel and the stunning magnetism of a very physical male.

She studied the dark planes of his impassive features, the clear golden eyes set beneath winged black brows and the savagely high cheekbones which lent such fierce strength to his face. Her gaze glossed over the stubborn jut of a decidedly Greek nose and the wide perfection of his narrow mouth before hurriedly falling away.

'I bet he's a voracious lover,' her mother had murmured throatily the first time she met him. 'He has an incredible sexual charge. I could feel it fifty feet away... any woman with red blood in her veins would. What's wrong with *you*?'

Jessica shivered. The red blood in her veins was chilling fast. Carlo was so cold. Although he betrayed nothing visually, she could feel that. And for some reason she couldn't understand that made her feel physically cold and threatened.

Suddenly the silence was something she might drown in and she leapt into speech. 'Why did you invite me here?'

'Take off your coat.'

Her tongue crept out and moistened her dry lower lip. 'I'm not staying——'

'Go, then,' he murmured with a dismissive flick of one lean hand. 'You waste my time——'

Her teeth clenched. She undid her sash, dropped the coat off her shoulders and cast it aside. 'I asked you why you invited me here.'

'I wanted to look at you.' Burnished golden eyes skimmed over her slender figure, resting on the surprisingly full thrust of her breasts above her tiny waist and sliding with insulting cool down over the feminine swell of her hips.

Jessica had never been at ease with her own body. Her voluptuous curves and her silver-blonde hair drew male eyes like beacons. Both attracted the wrong kind of male attention. She looked like her mother and she despised that awareness. If she hadn't possessed a distressingly opulent shape and unnaturally bright hair which ironically was entirely natural, she would never have caught Carlo Saracini's attention six years ago.

Her eyes glittered like brilliant amethysts as she withstood his inspection with her chin as high as she could hold it.

'Would you like a drink?' he drawled.

'No, thank you.'

He poured himself a glass of champagne. 'I hate to celebrate alone but I understand that you're afraid of touching alcohol around me. I'm surprised you're still that naïve,' he remarked softly.

'What are you celebrating?' She ignored the dig about alcohol, drawing on every scrap of icy dignity she possessed.

'You're a widow,' he delivered with smooth emphasis.

Jessica was shattered by his candour, brutally reminded that Carlo had no inhibitions and, similarly, little respect for ordinary standards of decent behaviour.

'My father——'

Carlo straightened to his full six feet three inches and shifted a silencing hand, dark golden eyes gleaming over her pallor. 'He stole from me and from his employees. We know that. Do we really need to discuss it?'

'Do you have to be so callous?' Jessica demanded, abruptly unfreezing from the spot to move forward in unconscious appeal. 'He made a huge error of judgement——'

'The prisons are full of people who make huge errors,' Carlo incised, his nostrils flaring. 'Theft? Such a sordid crime and yet so personal——'

'P-personal?' Involuntarily, she stammered.

'It was for your sake alone that I bought Amory Engineering at an inflated price. What you might call a gesture of good faith towards your family——'

'Good faith?' A choked laugh fell from her lips as she studied him with unhidden loathing and disbelief. 'You don't know what good faith is. It was blackmail. You tried to put pressure on me by playing on my family's financial position——'

'I was demonstrating that I look after *my own*,' Carlo cut in with ruthless precision.

'*Your own*?' she repeated with revulsion. 'I was never yours!'

A winged ebony brow was elevated. 'You were mine the first moment our eyes met but you were too stupid and craven to face that reality——'

'How dare you!'

'How dare you enter this room where you lay with me and try to deny what happened here between us?' Carlo demanded with blistering contempt.

She wanted to hit him. She wanted to scream back from the depths of her humiliation. But she wouldn't allow herself to be drawn. 'My father——' she said very deliberately.

'Was the most cosseted employee I have ever had,' Carlo interrupted. 'I allowed him complete autonomy over a company which was no longer his and in return I expected loyalty, not common theft.'

'He can sell his house and pay back every penny!' Jessica swore furiously. 'Isn't that enough for you?'

'Your family home carries two mortgages. Why do you think he stole?' Carlo returned drily. 'I wish to hear no more on the subject.'

'He's desperately ashamed of himself.' Jessica hadn't known that the house was mortgaged. She concealed her dismay with difficulty.

'This subject bores me.' Carlo sent her a grim glance. 'I have no interest in your father except as a means to an end. You can't influence my judgement with sentimental pleas. There is no sentiment in business——'

'So you simply brought me here to gloat?' she gathered with flashing eyes and a look of glowing scorn. 'You make me sick, Carlo. I will stand by my father through whatever you throw at him——'

'You like weak men, don't you?' he said silkily. 'Men who need mothering and support, men who make you feel that you're the one in the driver's seat. Maybe if I'd wept and plucked violin strings instead of demanded, you would have come to me instead...'

'Don't be crass.' Jessica was trembling with a rage that was becoming increasingly hard to control. 'I would never have *come* to you. I hated you for your primitive macho outlook and——'

'I am not primitive.' The insertion was immensely quiet but the temperature had shot up. 'I have Greek blood.'

For a split-second she was tempted to laugh. So vast an amount of blatant pride and arrogance dwelt in that assurance. But then she clashed with golden eyes that burned with the ferocity of a tiger about to pounce and all desire to laugh was stolen from her. Instantly the alarm bells rang in a frantic peal inside her head. That ferocious, utterly terrifying temper... She found herself instinctively glancing round to measure the distance to the door.

'And you are not my equal. You proved that six years ago!' he shot at her. 'Most conclusively did you prove your stupidity——'

Her small hands clenched into fists. 'If you call me stupid just one more time, Carlo, I won't be responsible for what I do!'

'*Per Dio*,' he murmured with a brilliant, slashing smile. 'If I push a little more, will you rip off my shirt and beg me to take you the way you did the last time?'

'Dear God, how can you talk to me like that?'

'Easily. Then,' Carlo spread two very expressive hands, 'I have no respect for you. What did you expect?'

The rage was beginning to gain on her self-control. She was having a very tough time holding it in.

'You behaved like a whore——'

'You swine!' she positively spat at him, powered by a tremendous wave of aggression.

'You were true neither to me nor to Turner,' Carlo drawled with caustic bite. 'He offered marriage. I offered something less secure. You went for the wedding-ring. And you lost.'

'I married the man I loved... I didn't lose *anything*!' Jessica slung back hotly, her adrenalin pumping madly through her veins.

Carlo threw his darkly handsome head back and laughed uproariously. 'Are you telling me that you didn't think of me in the dark of night? That you didn't crave the passion I alone could give you? If you'd responded to him the way you responded to me, he'd have run away from you in terror!'

Jessica launched herself at him like a lioness. Two incredibly powerful hands snapped round her wrists and held her back. An insolent smile curved his hard mouth. 'You dress like a fifty-year-old spinster but you're a little animal at heart, aren't you, *cara*? I scratch the surface of that ladylike exterior and I find teeth and claws. I like that. It excites me——'

'You filthy swine...*shut up!*' she screamed.

'And it excites the hell out of you too!' Long fingers hauled her closer as she attempted to kick him. He caught both flailing hands in one large male hand and pinned them behind her back, forcing her closer, staring with sardonic amusement down into her blazing violet eyes and pressing a long muscular thigh against her stomach as she twisted and tried to apply a well-aimed knee. 'All that howling sexual frustration just begging to be released. I could take you now here...up against the wall, on the floor, anywhere and you'd love it!' he asserted with rawly offensive confidence. 'Is that what you want?'

CHAPTER TWO

'NEVER!' Jessica gasped breathlessly, searing his dark, savage visage with all the tortured fury of her ignominious and powerless position. 'The very idea of you touching me again makes me feel physically sick!'

'One lesson wasn't enough for you, was it?' Carlo murmured huskily, narrowed eyes raking over her outraged features. 'Don't you remember what it was like when I made love to you?'

'That wasn't love,' Jessica vented fiercely. 'That was *lust*!'

'And you have a problem with that... I don't,' Carlo confided in a black velvet purr. And then, with a sardonic laugh, he released her when she was least expecting the gesture and thrust her carelessly back from him.

Jessica was trembling and in considerable distress. She had lost control. Physical and mental control. And that terrified her. Six years ago, she had been twenty, barely out of the teen years and considerably more naïve and foolish than she considered herself to be now. The last few minutes were like a blackout inside her mind. She didn't want to examine them. He had made her so angry she had become violent and that knowledge literally filled her with shame and horror.

Her body felt peculiar. Her heartbeat was still madly accelerated. Her breasts were suddenly extraordinarily sensitive. She was maddeningly aware that the lace cup of her bra was chafing her nipples and that her skin felt stretched and tight. Horrified by what had happened to her body, she studied the floor, fighting to relocate her composure.

'Let's get down to business,' Carlo suggested drily. 'We've wasted enough time.'

'Business?' Her brow furrowed.

'I invited you here for one reason only. You *could* be of use to me. I need a woman to play a role. A woman I can trust to play that role to the best of her ability and do exactly as she's told. And I think that that woman could be you——'

Her lashes fluttered in bemusement. 'I don't think I follow.'

'If you are prepared to place yourself without question in my hands for a period, not exceeding three months, I will consider treating your father's offence with sympathy, understanding and forgiveness...' Carlo stated quietly.

Sympathy, understanding and forgiveness. Alien emotions where Carlo was concerned. Her temples were throbbing. Her concentration was blown. She studied him with perceptible incomprehension, temporarily drained of all emotion. She just didn't know what he was talking about.

'This role,' Carlo selected smoothly, letting champagne froth down into another glass. 'It would entail considerable intimacy——'

'Intimacy?' she whispered shakily.

Carlo slotted the glass into her nerveless fingers. He surveyed her with immense satisfaction. 'Intimacy,' he repeated lazily, making a sexual banquet of the word and the long-drawn-out syllables were like a set of taunting fingers on her spine.

'What...what exactly are you offering me?' Jessica framed jerkily.

'You would have to agree before I told you the details.' Carlo dealt her a cool, steady glance, silky black lashes low over hooded, very dark eyes.

'That's ridiculous.'

'Unusual.' Carlo shifted a broad shoulder in a slight shrug. 'But I don't trust you. Why should I? And it is not as though you have moral scruples, is it? And even if you had,' he pointed out, 'you do have your father to consider.'

She tensed, forcing herself to concentrate. 'Are you talking about some kind of job?'

Carlo's mouth curved wryly. 'You could call it that.'

'And would it entail breaking the law?' she prompted flatly.

'What do you take me for, *cara*?'

'Would it?' she persisted.

'No.'

Jessica cleared her throat. 'You mentioned intimacy...were you talking about sexual intimacy?' she pursued, tight-lipped and rigid. 'Or was that just your idea of a joke?'

His strong jawline hardened. 'There would be nothing remotely humorous about the exercise, that I can assure you. And yes, I was referring to sexual intimacy. The part you would play would not be credible without it.'

Dear heaven, why was she actually standing here listening to this nonsense? Her oval face set with distaste and rejection as her imagination ran absolutely rampant. Was he suggesting that she become some sort of business spy, sleeping with some competitor to gain information? An insane idea, but why else the secrecy? A kind of job that would last no longer than three months which would entail sex. How utterly revolting! A hysterical laugh clogged up her throat though. Her level of sexual experience lifted such a proposition to the heights of a tragicomic black joke...but then Carlo was not to know that.

Jessica threw back her shoulders. 'Clearly you need a hooker——'

'*Madre di Dio*...what are you saying to me?' Carlo shot her a black glance of naked hauteur. 'Are you crazy?

I need a woman who can at the very least behave like a lady——'

'And you don't know any?' Jessica cut in. 'Now why doesn't that surprise me? And how many beds are you expecting this *lady* to climb into at your request?'

Dark golden eyes narrowed. 'What the hell are you talking about?'

Jessica reddened, suddenly uncertain.

'The only bed you would be expected to warm would be mine,' Carlo spelt out very drily.

Jessica went white and looked back at him in disbelief. Setting down the untouched champagne, she reached for her coat with an unsteady hand. 'Quite out of the question,' she told him with bitter clarity. 'I have no intention of selling my body to keep my father out of prison! Why the cloak and dagger approach, Carlo? Couldn't you just have asked me to be your mistress? Well, the answer is no...no, no, *no*! I'd sooner take to the streets!'

Brilliant dark eyes raked over her impassively. 'Go, then...I have nothing more to say to you.'

'But I'm not finished yet,' Jessica asserted with venom. 'Six years ago, you came into my life like a dark shadow and you tried to destroy it. There is no human being alive whom I hate more than you! And why did you set out to wreck my life? Out of nothing more than overweening conceit, selfishness and lust. It didn't matter to you that I was engaged to another man or that I loved that man. It didn't matter that you might hurt him as much as you hurt me.'

'You hurt him, not I,' Carlo returned without emotion.

Jessica shuddered with the force of her own teeming emotions. 'You set out to ruin our relationship——'

'If you had truly loved him, I would have been without power. The power I had *you gave me*...'

Hot pink flushed her slanted cheekbones. 'I did not!'

'With every look, every breath you took in my radius. Your hunger drew me,' Carlo condemned without conscience.

'*No!*' She stared back at him in stark distress and reproach, her father's plight forgotten as he plunged her back into the past, heaping her with more guilt and an even greater sense of responsibility for all that had gone wrong.

'Did it give your ego a kick?' Carlo sent her a look of blazing contempt. 'You play with fire, you get burnt, *cara.*'

Jessica's knees felt like cotton wool. She was shattered by Carlo's view of what had happened between them. He was accusing her of having encouraged him when she had fought his ruthless pursuit every step of the way. Only at the last when she was at the very end of her strength had she failed.

'I came here and I shouldn't have come.' White and drawn, she turned away. 'We hate each other, Carlo. I don't think you realise the extent of the damage you did six years ago and I expect that even if you did you wouldn't care——'

'*You walked away from me...*'

And it was still there, an intensity of disbelief and banked-down fury. She couldn't understand the strength of his emotion after all this time. It wasn't as though Carlo Saracini had fallen in love with her. Right from the beginning, it had been a rawly sexual wanting on his side. The way he looked at her, the way he touched her, the way he talked to her. Predator and victim. Passion and pain. That was what he had offered her. And she hadn't walked away...she had run as if the hounds of hell were on her tail.

'I still don't think I deserve the offer you just made,' Jessica breathed not quite steadily. 'You sit there in your ivory tower, wrapped in all your money, and you have the sensitivity of a butcher where feelings are concerned.' Tears stung her amethyst eyes but she held her head proudly high.

'That is a gross untruth,' Carlo slashed back at her rawly.

'You walk over people. You manipulate them. You push them around. My father really liked you six years ago. You see, he couldn't see through you as I could. Oh, yes, he thought you were a hell of a guy!' she proffered in a choked voice of distaste. 'But you don't give a snap of your fingers for what he's going through now, do you? All you can see is an opportunity to humiliate me further. And I will not give you that weapon, Carlo. You see, I have my pride too.'

He was pale beneath his naturally olive skintone but he wouldn't give an inch. And she hadn't expected him to. Censure rarely came his way. In receipt of it, he silently seethed, presumably thinking it beneath his dignity to defend himself against such charges.

Eyes as flaming gold as the heart of a fire burned her face. 'Were you happy with him?'

On her passage to the door, she froze and slowly turned. He hadn't absorbed a thing she had said. Pain dug lines of stress into her face. He was asking about Simon. She looked away. 'He was my best friend,' she said finally.

'And this... this being a best friend is your ideal of marriage?' Carlo demanded, his usually fluent English curiously letting him down.

No, but it was what she had ended up with, she reflected sadly. Her troubled eyes slid back to him and collided with questioning gold and something twisted tight deep down inside her stomach. The atmosphere fairly throbbed with undertones. She stopped breathing, was sentenced to sudden stillness, every bone in her body pulling taut. For a split-second, she experienced the most extraordinary physical pull in his direction and resisted it with every last remaining drop of self-discipline. But that split-second shook her inside out.

'I would have been your lover, your soul, your survival,' Carlo gritted, and the anger was there, the anger she had feared, suddenly flaring up at her without warning in a blazing wall of antagonism that made her step back. Burnished golden eyes alive with derision and fury bit into her with a look as physical as a blow.

'Get out of here,' Carlo told her roughly. 'Get out of here before I lose my temper and show you just how sensitive I can be!'

Jessica required only that one invitation. On unsteady legs, she backed out in haste. Out in the corridor, she closed her eyes and breathed in slowly and deeply. She felt bereft, alone, wretched, and the sensations were intense. Carlo confused her, cast her into turmoil. He always had. They were opposites in every way but just for a moment... for a strange and highly disturbing moment she had recognised an utterly inexplicable pang of empathy. She had wanted to put her arms round him.

Crazy, unbelievable, just one of those mad tricks of the mind when one's emotions were on a high, she translated inwardly. After all, would she pet a sabre-toothed tiger plotting to put her on his dinner menu? But she could not escape the feeling that she had hurt him. And yet wasn't that what she had always wanted to do?

When she was with Carlo Saracini she didn't know herself. It had always been that way. With other people she was introverted and quiet, never bitchy or hot-tempered and certainly not violent. Dear heaven, she thought as she recalled the manner in which she had launched herself at him like a screaming shrew. He drew out everything that was bad in her character. He made her feel as though she could turn into a woman like her mother... wasn't that what frightened her the most?

She got into her car without remembering leaving the hotel. She didn't start the engine. She stared out the windscreen unseeingly. The way she had felt when he touched her six years ago still haunted her. And every so often she *made* herself draw those memories out to reinforce her own disgust and shame. Not only did she look like her mother, she had found that she could *behave* like her too. That had been the most devastating discovery of all. That there was this weakness inside her, this ability to forget everything ... loyalty, self-restraint, even love ... and lose all control in a man's arms.

Sometimes, Jessica had even told herself that she ought to be grateful for that sordid incident with Carlo. She had been afraid then that if she didn't remain constantly on her guard, virtually policing even her thoughts, she too might easily turn into a slut. If it hadn't been for that noise next door, Carlo wouldn't have stopped, she knew that. Sex was a terrifyingly powerful force if you knew yourself to be as vulnerable as Jessica felt herself to be. One weak moment in the vicinity of a male like Carlo and that would be that. She had been incredibly lucky to escape unscathed.

Only somehow, she thought now on a tide of bitter pain, it had never occurred to her that she might be just as unscathed six years on, after five years of marriage. Untouched by human hand. A virgin, no less. And wouldn't Carlo just love to know that, she reflected painfully, shuddering at the very idea. He would find it hilarious.

Jessica drifted out of her thoughts to find herself sitting shivering inside a very cold car with all the windows fogged up. She drove off but somewhere down deep in her mind was an image of Carlo as she had last seen him in the hotel suite. Angry, contemptuous ... *bitter*? What the heck did he have to be bitter about? Had he really imagined she would accept that grossly insulting offer? Three months in Carlo's bed, working out her penance for daring to marry another man. What a monumental ego he must have! And the utterly peculiar way he had gone about making that offer... Her head was thumping again, tension twisting through her like a steel wire.

It was too late to go barging in on her father. Tomorrow morning first thing, she would be on his doorstep, and if he hadn't seen a lawyer yet she would see that he did. It was a crisis and she was good in a crisis. For years it seemed her life had lurched from one crisis to another.

She was about to phone her father when the doorbell went. She peered through the peephole and recognised the broad, weathered features of the heavily built man on the other side of the door.

'Dr Guthrie...?' Her brow furrowed. Henry Guthrie was one of her father's oldest friends. He and his wife ran a private nursing home.

'I tried to ring you earlier but you were out,' he proffered.

'What's wrong?' she demanded, anxiously scanning his troubled face.

'Your father's going to stay with us for a day or two until I can get him sorted out——'

'But why...I mean, I gather you know what's happened...but what's the matter with him?' Jessica prompted sickly.

Henry Guthrie sighed. 'Gerald's been receiving treatment for depression for some months now——'

She paled. 'He didn't tell me...'

'He's been quietly going off the rails ever since your mother died.'

She shut her eyes and groaned. Four months ago, they had received news of her mother's death in a car crash. From the day she walked out until the day she died, neither Jessica nor her father had had any contact with Carole. Her mother hadn't wanted any contact. She had wiped them both out of her life and had embarked on a new life abroad.

'But he seemed to take it so *well*,' she protested shakily.

'Didn't it ever occur to you that he took it too well?' the older man murmured. 'I think that he still hoped that she would come back. But when she died, he had to finally face that she was gone. That's when the depression came and the gambling started. Now I understand he's got himself in one hell of a mess——'

'Yes,' she whispered, tears stinging her eyes.

'He just can't cope with it, Jess,' Dr Guthrie sighed. 'He took some sleeping tablets this afternoon——'

Jessica gasped at him in horror. 'He did what?'

'Not enough to kill him but then, he didn't have enough. His housekeeper found him lying in the hall and thought he'd had a heart attack...'

Jessica collapsed down on the sofa behind her, sick to her stomach, and bowed her head.

'She rang me. I saw the tablets and contacted his own doctor, worked out how many he must have taken and between us...well, we decided the nursing home would be a better choice than the local hospital.'

Tracks of moisture ran unchecked down her cheeks. She wanted to thank the older man for exercising that discretion but she couldn't find her voice.

'Now when he came to, he swore he hadn't been trying to harm himself. He said he was just desperate to stop his mind going round and round and get some sleep and when the first pills didn't do the trick, he took a few more...'

'Do you b-believe him?'

'I'll know better what to think in a few days when we've talked some more,' he confessed wryly. 'Well...now I'm here to ask you how to get in touch with this character, Saracini——'

'Carlo?' she gasped.

'Do you think he'd see me? I want to tell him that Gerald needs criminal charges right now like he needs a hole in the head!' he delivered grimly.

Jessica was barely thinking straight. But one awareness dominated the morass of emotions tearing her apart. Tonight she might have lost her father. And even if it hadn't been a suicide attempt, in his current condition, who was to say he mightn't make such an attempt this week or next week or the week after? If he wasn't coping now, how could she expect him to cope when the police were involved and the news of his disgrace leaked out? How could he handle all the horrors still to come?

She cleared her throat. 'There aren't going to be any criminal charges. I...I saw Carlo tonight and he was very understanding——'

'He wasn't very understanding when he had Gerald tossed out of the building!'

'I explained how much strain Dad had been under. There won't be any court case,' she repeated unsteadily, her slender hands twisting together as she made her decision.

'But what about the money? I gather that Gerald has no hope of paying all of it back...'

'Carlo is prepared to write it off——'

'He must be a very decent sort of man.' Dr Guthrie shook his head. 'I honestly thought he would want to nail your father's hide to the wall as an example to the rest of his employees...'

An inward quaking at that particular image assailed Jessica. She tasted cold fear but this time it was not only for her father, it was for herself as well.

The older man smothered a yawn and stood up. 'I'll pass on the good news to Gerald.'

'I'll come and see him tomorrow.'

Dr Guthrie grimaced. 'Would you be terribly hurt if I advised you to give him a couple of days to get himself together again?'

'No,' she lied.

'He feels he's let you down and I don't think he wants you to see him until he has himself under control again.'

'No problem,' she said stiffly.

'He still has a lot to handle, Jess. He's lost his job and his self-respect.'

As soon as the older man had gone, Jessica dialled the Deangate Hotel with clumsy fingers. She asked for Carlo's suite. He answered the call with a growl of impatience in his voice.

'It's me . . .' she said tightly. 'I've changed my mind.'

Silence buzzed on the line for long seconds. It went on and on and on while she trembled at her end of the phone with a heady mix of fear and despair. Maybe Carlo had never expected her to accept . . . maybe Carlo had been playing some sort of game with her.

'I'll send a car over to collect you.' There was no emotion whatsoever in his response. She couldn't believe her ears.

'When?'

'Now.'

'*Now*?' she echoed incredulously.

'Now,' he repeated, his accent more pronounced than she had ever heard it. 'I waited six years. I won't wait one hour or one day longer.'

'I can't come over to your hotel at this time of night,' Jessica gasped.

'Why not?' His deep, dark voice thickened audibly. 'You won't be going home again . . .'

Jessica was shattered. *Now . . . tonight*?

'And if you don't come tonight, the deal's off.'

'That's totally unreasonable!'

'But what I want,' Carlo asserted.

'You can't always have what you want——'

'Can't I?' He laughed softly and the phone went dead.

CHAPTER THREE

JESSICA kept the car waiting an hour. She packed as though she was going away for the weekend. In the back of her mind, a voice kept on saying, You can't be doing this... you can't have agreed. The unknown beckoned with all the welcome of a black, endless tunnel. She lifted a photo of Simon off the nightstand and stared at it tautly. It had been taken the day he opened the photographic studio. Unusually, he was wearing a suit. A slim, fair man of medium height with gentle brown eyes.

'It doesn't matter to me... that sort of thing is really not important,' Simon had soothed when she sobbed out her shame and despair after that dreadful afternoon when she had almost ended up sharing Carlo Saracini's bed. 'Of course I forgive you.'

Simon and his family had moved next door when she was ten and he was fourteen. He had been the odd one out in his large, extrovert family. Quiet and unambitious, his greatest interest wildlife photography. Simon had been an oddity to his rugby-mad father and brothers. And Jessica had been a lonely child, painfully conscious from an early age that her mother had no time for her or her father.

Simon had heard Jessica sobbing her heart out in the summer house the day she came home early from school and saw Carole half-undressed with a strange man. Simon had climbed over the wall and she had been so shocked by what she had seen that she had told him. He had been very kind and comforting. He had put his arm round her and listened, showing her the easy affection she craved.

The adult world had come to her door that day. Simon had explained that she mustn't tell her father or anyone else about that accidental glimpse. He had been naïve too in his assumption that her mother didn't make a habit of that sort of thing. Jessica hadn't been very much older before she had learnt that there was always another man in Carole's life and that her father simply tried to pretend not to know about those men.

Indeed she had soon realised that her mother's frequent affairs were food for the juiciest gossip in town. That knowledge had been an agonising humiliation to live with during the sensitive teen years.

And throughout it all, Simon had been there for her. Her best friend, her adolescent hero. By the time she had reached seventeen, both their families had begun to view them as inseparable. But, looking back, she now recalled that Simon had never talked of love or marriage or children with her, not until his family and other people began teasing them repeatedly about when they planned to tie the knot.

He had actually gone down to work in London for over a year, coming back on only odd weekends, and she had thought she was losing him, had actually wondered if Simon had ever been hers to lose, if indeed he was striving to break away from the popular belief that they were childhood sweethearts destined to marry.

Then out of the blue, the Christmas she was eighteen, Simon had asked her to get engaged. Even when he'd carefully stressed his wish for a long engagement, Jessica had been ecstatic, convinced that together they were a match made in heaven. There was nothing she could not tell Simon, nothing, it seemed, that they could not discuss. In every way they had seemed to complement each other, unlike her parents who didn't have a single thought in common.

Dear God, but she had been so innocent, she reflected now, tucking the photo into her overnight bag. Blind right to the bitter end. When had it finally occurred to her that the average male would have lifted the roof when his bride-to-be very nearly fell into another man's bed a week before the wedding? Her betrayal *should* have mattered to Simon. It *should* have been important to him. And forgiveness *should* not have come so quickly and easily to his lips. Ironically, Jessica had been far more upset than Simon had been. She had wanted to cancel the wedding but Simon had pleaded with her, telling her how much he needed her, and in the end, she had allowed herself to be persuaded...

The limousine ate up the miles back to the hotel and with every mile her tension mounted another unbearable notch. Not only was she being forced to face a savage humiliation, but also to accept the necessity of bargaining with Carlo for her father's sake. She did not yet know if Carlo would even agree to what she had already promised in his name.

Jessica didn't approach the night receptionist. With the chauffeur bringing up the rear with her bag and waving away the proffered attentions of the porter, she was terrified of being asked where she was going and why she wasn't signing the hotel register. The man flicked her a glance, said nothing, and then her pale cheeks fired on a worse thought. Did he think she was a call-girl? Didn't hotels discreetly ignore those sort of comings and goings?

A waiter opened the door of Carlo's suite.

Carlo was standing by the fireplace, talking on the phone in rapid Italian. He looked past Jessica and made a signal to his chauffeur, briefly connected with Jessica's taut stance several steps inside the room and said carelessly in an aside, 'I was about to dine without you, *cara*.'

Her gaze fell on the table exquisitely set for two. She hadn't eaten since breakfast but she did not feel hungry. The waiter lit the candelabra, dimmed the lights and then uncorked the wine and hovered.

Carlo cast the phone aside and crossed the room in a couple of long strides. Confident hands undid the sash at her waist, parted her coat and slid it off her tense shoulders as if she were a doll to be undressed.

'Pour the wine and leave us,' he murmured to the waiter, a hand touching her narrow back as he walked her to the table, tugged out a chair and sat her down.

With a not quite steady hand she reached for her glass as soon as it was filled.

'One glass only,' Carlo decreed with dark satire. 'I would hate to be accused of getting you drunk a second time.'

Heat crawled up her slender throat. She couldn't meet his eyes. She couldn't think of anything beyond the fact that she was here in Carlo's suite and expected to share his bed tonight. 'I think the receptionist thought I was a call-girl.'

'Surely not?' Carlo parried silkily. 'A high-class hooker would never be so badly dressed.'

Her teeth clenched. 'I didn't come here to be insulted.'

'I think you came here to take whatever I choose to hand out,' Carlo flicked back, skimming her taupe skirt and blouse with a curled lip. 'When you kept me waiting, I mistakenly assumed you were dressing up for the occasion——'

A choked laugh that was no laugh at all escaped her. 'What occasion?'

'I ordered all your favourite foods.'

So he had. She hadn't noticed. He had to have a phenomenal memory.

'I remember everything about you.'

He sounded as if he expected a round of applause.

'We have to talk about my father,' she opened in a rush.

'You haven't met my eyes once since you entered this room.'

Involuntarily, she clashed with glittering gold alive with impatience above a set jawline. Evidently she was not delivering the required responses.

'This won't work if you can't do better than this,' he said drily, unfeelingly.

'Don't threaten me...' she warned tautly, great violet eyes nailed to his hard dark features. 'I function even less efficiently under threat. Now...can we talk about my father?'

'I prefer to eat to the accompaniment of *light* conversation.'

Her gaze damned him to hell and back. She dug into the pâté with sudden appetite. She worked through the next two courses without speaking unless forced. If anyone lost their appetite it was Carlo, finally thrusting his plate away with an imprecation and tossing aside his napkin as he rose from the table.

'You sulk like a little girl.'

'I am not sulking, Carlo.' Jessica embarked slowly on her dessert, it having long since occurred to her that the longer she spent eating, the longer she stayed out of the bedroom. 'You wanted me here. I came. You wanted me to eat. I am eating.'

'I won't prosecute your father.' The statement was coolly unemotional.

'He can't pay back the money——'

'He must,' Carlo's tough jawline set hard. 'The money must be returned.'

'*How*?' she demanded bitterly. 'He has no job and he's not likely to get another one. And even if he sells everything he has, he will still owe you money.'

'I will give him another position, then.'

Startled by that most unexpectedly generous offer, she stared at him. 'Where?'

'Not here. He needs a fresh start for this second chance. Leave it with me,' he drawled. 'I will find him something.'

'And the money?' she prompted.

'He repays,' Carlo repeated grimly. 'If he is as sorry and as ashamed as you protest, he will want to repay it. He will not wish to be further in my debt.'

'But——?'

'In addition,' Carlo cut across her interruption drily, 'the offer of continuing employment will be conditional on his agreement to seek help for his addiction——'

'He's not addicted!' Jessica jumped to her father's defence.

'Any man capable of gambling so far above his own income is an addict. He requires therapy to ensure he can withstand future temptation. Now, are you satisfied?' he demanded shortly, dismissively, making her suspect that he had conceded more than he had planned to concede.

Yet Jessica had hoped for more. She had wanted the debt wiped out as she had promised Dr Guthrie. Whether it was unreasonable or not, she wanted every practical cause of stress removed from her father's path. 'You're getting me pretty cheap, aren't you?' she said shakily and then, the instant she saw the dark fury leap into his set features, she wished she had bitten her tongue and stayed silent.

'You want to go on the payroll for three months for sharing my bed?' Carlo threw back at her with a flash of even white teeth. 'A contract maybe, complete with severance pay and an assurance that you retain any jewellery or clothes that I buy you? OK, that is fine by me.' He moved an expressive brown hand in a gesture that made it very clear that it was anything but fine with him. 'I have heard of such contracts in America. But do tell me now up-front, what price do *you* put on that perfect body of yours?'

She wondered sickly whether, if someone handcuffed his talkative hands behind his back, he would still be able to articulate. 'You know that's not what I meant.'

'Do I?' Nostrils flaring, he surveyed her with derisive dark eyes.

She rested her brow down on the heel of one unsteady hand. It was almost one in the morning. That wouldn't bother Carlo. He had reserves of energy unknown to less advantaged mortals. She wanted to go to bed but the prospect of bed was fraught with far more alarming possibilities than she could face. 'At this moment,' she whispered, 'all I need to know is what you expect from me over the next three months.'

Silence fell. Since silence was rare from Carlo's corner, she looked up.

Carlo cleared his throat, tension thrumming from his poised stance by the window. 'I want you to pretend to be my fiancée——'

She couldn't hide her astonishment. 'Why?'

'I have my reasons,' he parried, the anger gone and replaced by a set gravity which disturbed her.

'I don't see why you can't tell me——'

'I will tell you only this,' he breathed shortly, his golden eyes grim and distant as he studied her. 'I have been estranged from my father for some years and now he is dying. I wish to spend some time with him and, to facilitate this wish, I require a fiancée to accompany me to his home.'

Shaken by the unemotional explanation, Jessica studied him in turn, helplessly, maddeningly curious about why a pretend fiancée should be a necessary requirement of such a visit. She presumed he was intending a reconciliation with his father. Why muddy the water with the presence of a fake fiancée, for goodness' sake? Especially when his father was dying... a stranger would surely be even less welcome in those circumstances?

Her smooth brow furrowed. 'Once you told me that you had no family.'

'In the sense of the true meaning of the word "family",' he stressed, 'that was the truth. My mother died when I was fourteen. I was sent off to school. My father remarried and after a while he chose to forget my existence. He had his life and I my own until, some years ago, we met again at his instigation...' His strong features shadowed, his eyes night-dark and impassive. 'And what happened between us then severed all familial ties,' he completed harshly.

There were so many questions she wanted answered that she was on the edge of her seat. 'What happened?' she finally prompted in frustration when it was clear that he had no intention of continuing.

Carlo cast her a sardonic smile. 'Like all women, you are incurably inquisitive. Knowledge is a weapon in a calculating woman's hands. Do you think I don't know that?' he gibed, scanning her sudden pallor with derision. 'I don't spill my guts to anyone, *cara*...I never have and I never will.'

He made her feel like a peeping tom with a door slammed shut on her prying fingers. It hurt, humiliated.

'I only require one thing from you. A good act. My father is not a stupid man. He will not be easily deceived.'

'I don't want to deceive anyone.'

'That's why we really will be lovers by the time we arrive. Intimacy, like sexual chemistry, is something that can be *felt*,' Carlo asserted with husky conviction. 'The sole deception will be the pretence of love and of course...my intention to marry you.'

Lovers.... She stiffened helplessly at the threat of what was yet to come. Arrive where? she might have asked, had not her nervous tension been too heightened for her to care at that moment. But still she longed to know why he was prepared to put on such an elaborate deception for his father's benefit. And then cynicism suggested his motive. His father was dying, presumably a wealthy man. Was Saracini Senior attaching conditions to his heir's inheritance? Was he demanding that Carlo settle down and marry? Could anyone be that old-fashioned these days? And was cold, hard cash at the foot of Carlo's deception?

'I think it's time we went to bed.'

Jessica froze. Carlo reached down for her hands and drew her up slowly, almost tauntingly. 'You're trembling... why? You've been married for years; you are not without experience.' Predictably, the reference to her marital status darkened his glittering eyes, hardened his mouth and roughened his syllables.

'That doesn't make any difference!'

'*Dio* ...' he swore, running a familiar forefinger down the buttons lining her silk blouse and then pausing to flick up to the top one and slide it loose, allowing himself access to the shadowed valley between her breasts. 'Of course it makes a difference. Were you a faithful wife?'

He towered over her. His broad shoulders blocked out the light. She felt trapped and cornered and told herself that that was why she could barely get air into her lungs. A blunt fingertip, very dark against her pale skin, hovered and she stopped breathing altogether. 'Of c-course I was——'

'Really? I find that hard to believe,' Carlo murmured softly as his fingers hit on the next button.

'Why?' she gasped half an octave higher.

'You weren't faithful before the wedding... why afterwards?' he prompted. 'If you had been my bride, I would have killed you. I certainly wouldn't have gone ahead and still married you.'

I would have killed you. Said softly, conversationally but with incredible certainty. A buzzing sound filled her eardrums as a hand brushed across the swell of her breasts. All of a sudden she felt light-headed and dizzy but her breasts felt full and heavy.

'Did you tell him about what happened between us?' Carlo asked.

'Yes!'

'So you told him the whole truth and nothing but the truth. I bet you didn't,' Carlo guessed with cruel and merciless amusement. 'I doubt if you gave him a blow-by-blow account...he'd never have recovered from it.'

'I don't want to talk about this!' Jessica slung at him tremulously and then, belatedly registering that her blouse was now hanging open, she backed away from him so fast, the side table behind her dug painfully into her hipbone. 'Carlo...I met you again less than five hours ago——'

'Who's counting? I'm not. I would have been at this stage four and a half hours ago if you hadn't been so stubborn——'

'That's disgusting!' she threw back in raw outrage.

'But truthful...don't you know yet how the male mind works?'

She was starting to find out. Carlo was surveying her with smouldering golden eyes, hot with unhidden desire. And the sexual charge her mother had once mentioned was like fireworks in the heavy atmosphere. She edged round the table beneath that tracking, utterly ruthless gaze. 'Carlo...please...not tonight...I mean——' the tip of her pink tongue snaked out to moisten her lower lip '—I mean, you can't really want to do this——'

'I do.' He bent down and shattered what remained of her fast-fleeing composure by letting his own tongue follow the path her own had taken along the full curve of her sultry lower lip, and heat surged between her thighs in a sensation long buried but never forgotten. She leapt back as though he had struck her and sent a lamp flying, her heart thumping like a jack-hammer against her breastbone.

He ignored the crash and caught her arm before she could busy herself reaching down for the broken pieces.

'I want a bath!' she exclaimed in desperation.

'And maybe you'd like me to go downstairs and smoke even though I don't smoke while you prepare yourself for bed like some blushing bride!' Carlo whipped back with lancing satire.

'Yes... what a good idea,' Jessica slung back at him bitterly. 'And maybe if you're very lucky you can find a whore in the bar, because clearly that's the only kind of woman you're accustomed to!' she completed with the shrill edge of hysteria in her shaking voice.

An electrifying silence fell. Carlo dropped her arm as though she had burnt him. Beneath her distraught gaze, he had tautened. Dark colour had highlighted his blunt cheekbones. 'Is that how you think I am treating you?' he gritted back at her.

'What do you think?' After that one explosion, Jessica was drained.

'That was not my intention.' He released his breath in a hiss.

Dully, she looked back at him, her lack of conviction in that assurance clearly visible.

'I'll go downstairs,' Carlo intoned flatly. 'I suppose I may hope that when I return, you will not have broken out into a rash or got blind drunk in my absence.'

'I beg your pardon?'

'Cary Grant and Doris Day... *That Touch of Mink*,' Carlo supplied sardonically. 'Haven't you ever seen that movie?'

'I'm afraid not,' she admitted tightly.

'I don't think I'll buy a video. You're doing just great on your own.'

And he was gone. And she couldn't quite work out how she had managed the feat. Smothering a yawn, she wandered into the bedroom, wondered if he realised that his biggest challenge would be keeping her awake. She rooted through her bag, dug out what she required and went into the bathroom without once looking at the bed.

Maybe he would meet some loose woman down in the bar.

Carlo was very, very good-looking. Funny, how she had sort of blocked that out over the years. Along with so much else. The cliff edge excitement he generated. The swift, volatile changes of mood. She didn't want to think about that afternoon six years ago. The turmoil, the passion, the sobbing utterly soul-shattering pleasure of his mouth and his hands on her body. Briefly she closed her eyes, her skin flaming. She really hadn't realised that the episode could have been anything that special on Carlo's scale of experience.

But evidently it had been. Otherwise why would he be so blatantly impatient to get her into bed? Then, on his terms, nothing very much had happened that long-ago day. A few heated caresses, a little disarranged clothing. But their lovemaking had not gone to its natural conclusion. Carlo had been deprived of that ultimate triumph. And had she come across as some sort of raving sex bomb? She crept into the enormous bed as warmly clad as a great-granny ready for the Blitz in the middle of the night, sheathed from throat to toe in brushed cotton. Why should she make it easy for him?

Tears burned her eyes and crept slowly down her cheeks into the pillow. It was sheer farce... all of it. You are not without experience, Carlo had blithely assumed. A sob tore painfully at her throat. Six years ago she had honestly believed that she had a terribly low sex-drive. Simon had confined himself to occasional rather chaste kisses. Simon had never asked for more. And she had decided that in that field they were as well suited as in every other. Sex did not play a part in their relationship before their marriage. She had been proud of that fact, certain that their bonds were built on far more sturdy foundations than those formed by couples in the heat of passion.

It was frighteningly ironic that Carlo had found her an unbearable temptation then. She just hadn't had a clue how to handle that. It had been an entirely new experience to meet a male who couldn't take his eyes off her, who would use the smallest excuse to touch her and who could turn her scarlet over a dinner table in company just by looking at her.

Yes... Carlo had *wanted* her. It had been Simon who hadn't wanted her. Simon who got exceedingly drunk on their wedding-night and who continued to drink throughout their fancy honeymoon in the Caribbean without consummating their marriage.

Jessica had gone through hell, reading his lack of interest and his drunkenness as her punishment for her shameless behaviour with Carlo. Guilt had tortured her into a ceaseless circle of blame and unending mortification. It had torn her apart night after night... the belief that she was reaping exactly what she deserved and that she had hurt Simon so badly that he couldn't even bring himself to touch her.

Who did you talk to about something so deeply personal and private? Simon had refused to talk about it, had withdrawn into a shell if she'd dared, and once or twice had taken off for days on end to avoid the subject. Her best friend had stopped being her best friend and become a moody, rarely sober stranger. It took her an incredibly long time to realise that Simon did not want her as a man wanted a woman and that, if she accepted that status quo, he was quite happy to live in a sham marriage and go back to being her best friend again.

She fell asleep wondering how long Carlo would devote to not smoking downstairs and whether he was already regretting their agreement. Regardless, she slept like a log, flattened by complete exhaustion.

And Carlo laughed with a rich appreciation that would have stunned her when he came back upstairs.

CHAPTER FOUR

JESSICA woke up from a long, dreamless sleep, gloriously relaxed. And then she opened her eyes. Carlo was less than six inches away. Dark golden eyes raked mockingly over her startled face. Relaxation vanished. Tension took its place.

'I don't think a woman has ever fallen asleep waiting for me before. You could be seriously bad for my ego——'

Jessica sat up with a falsely bright smile. 'Gosh, is that the time?' she gasped. 'Why didn't you wake me?'

Carlo dealt her a genuinely amused smile that quite transformed his powerful dark features. He anchored one hand in the tumbled fall of her silver hair before she could take evasive action. 'Don't worry about it. You're not in an all-girls dorm and sleeping late doesn't mean you miss breakfast,' he murmured, deliberately mimicking her schoolgirlish speech. 'Why did I ever call you stupid?'

Breathlessly, Jessica attempted to keep some space between them. 'I don't know.'

'You outgunned Doris Day last night,' he said softly, appreciatively. 'You stitched me up like a professional. I went out of here feeling like a cross between an oversexed and clumsy teenager and a complete bastard.'

'If the c-cap fits——'

His free hand curved to one slanted cheekbone, his gaze probing her wide violet eyes intently. 'And then you got into bed and slept like the dead. When you're asleep with your hair lying over the pillows, you look about sixteen. And incredibly untouched...' His husky voice deepened. 'Like a story-book princess. The day we met, you looked just like that lying on the road in a white summer dress with a lace collar. Then you opened your eyes and they were the colour of pansies after the rain ... *Madre di Dio*, I never wanted any woman in my life as I wanted you then!'

His deep, rich voice had a hypnotic quality that made her quiver. His palm felt warm against her cheekbone and her feathery lashes dropped low over her gaze, screening her sudden confusion from him. Every breath she inhaled seemed inadequate.

'I never had to fight for a woman before either ... but I love to be challenged and you made yourself a challenge with your frigid little smiles and your icy stares,' he told her. 'I knew that that wasn't the real Jessica. It was an act, a deception——'

'No!' she objected shakily. 'You saw something that wasn't there, a woman you created in your own mind, who never existed except in your imagination!'

'She existed here in this bed. She came alive in my arms. Passionate, fearless and irresistible. And I want her back again.'

Jerkily, she ducked her head away, but he wouldn't let her escape his hold. Her angry eyes clashed with suddenly thunderous gold and the long fingers in her silky hair tightened their grip. 'You are very stubborn,' he grated.

'And you're an egotistical jerk! I won't give you what you want. I'll play the part of your fiancée but the acting stops at the bedroom door,' Jessica slammed back at him, imperious in her fury.

'Like hell it will.' Carlo's enunciation was succinct.

'You want your pound of flesh?' Jessica demanded hotly. 'OK, take it!' She wrenched her hair free of his hold, flung herself flat on the bed again and said, 'Well, what are you waiting for?'

She tensed as his dark head lowered, eyes wide glimmering with defiance and scorn, breathing stilled. He wouldn't get any enjoyment out of it, she promised herself. If his idea of entertainment was making love to an inanimate body, let him go ahead.

Carlo took her mouth in an explosion of silencing heat, his dark head blocking out the light, his hands on her shoulders hard and rough. The heat was like a red-hot wire shooting through her and she gripped his arms frantically in a last-ditch attempt to break the connection. But he wouldn't let her go.

Her hands curled into fists and struck blindly out at his chest. In response, he darted a powerful hand under her limbs and flattened her to the bed. There was a rich, enveloping darkness beckoning behind her closed eyelids and she knew what it was and she fought it, struggling for breath, for control, for anything that would wipe out the sensations he was forcing her to feel.

But her body was treacherous in pursuit of those same sensations. Her nipples tautened into tight little buds, her thighs trembled and every inch of her quivered with anticipation. Excitement was taking over in hot, drugging little spirals that peaked as he stabbed his tongue deep into the moist interior of her mouth. Her hands tangled in his hair and she kissed him back, passionately and wildly, twisting up to him to get closer.

Hard hands wrenched the nightdress from her shoulders, down her arms, effectively imprisoning her, and she couldn't bear it, her hands tugging for freedom from the sleeves. But no sooner had she freed herself than he pinned her wrists to the sheet with an earthy sound of amusement.

The tip of his tongue flicked over the thrust of one swollen nipple and a sob of tortured sound escaped her. His lips enclosed the aching bud slowly, teasingly, and her back arched, her teeth gritting. 'No!' she almost sobbed.

'Yes...' Carlo said thickly, exploring the proud swell of her flesh with his mouth and his tongue and his teeth until she was torn from that last shred of control and frantic only for continuance.

He released her hands and eased her out of her nightdress in one smooth movement. Long, sure fingers caressed her now tender breasts, playing on the sensitivity he had awakened, and a low moan of growing frustration escaped her. Dragging him down to her, she found his mouth again for herself, a long sigh of pleasure torn from her as the black curls of hair on his chest rubbed an abrasive course against her erect nipples.

A blunt forefinger traced the length of one slender thigh and she trembled, jerked as he slid his hand over the flat, silky skin of her belly. It was as if a hot wire were tightening inside her. She couldn't stay still. He made love to her mouth slowly, erotically, every thrust of his tongue making her quiver with unbearable need. She gripped his shoulders, felt the heavy thud of his heartbeat against her, and craved more, shuddering with wave after wave of raw excitement as he lazily trailed one hand through the silvery curls at the apex of her thighs.

He lifted his head and looked down at her hectically flushed face and nibbled teasingly at the reddened curve of her lower lip. She was pitched on an agonising high of arousal as his fingertips flirted with the smooth skin of one inner thigh, maddeningly refusing to touch her where she ached to be touched.

'Please...' she panted, lost to everything but the screaming demands of her own body.

'Are you begging me?' Carlo whispered in a black velvet undertone, his breath fanning her cheek, burnished golden eyes scanning glazed amethyst.

'Carlo...' She trembled against him.

'Tell me.' His dark head lowered and his carnal mouth found an incredibly sensitive spot below one small ear, sending shivers of hot, burning need running through her.

'Don't stop!' She didn't recognise the desperate edge in her own voice.

And suddenly she was free. Carlo lounged back against the pillows and watched her with hooded, calculating, dark-as-night eyes. Wildly disorientated, she stared back, not understanding, not comprehending anything but the painful ache of her own hotly aroused body.

'Never dare to tell me again that you don't want me,' Carlo murmured softly, sibilantly, studying her with chilling detachment. 'I can make you want me. You're a very sensual woman. You were made for passion——'

Too late she understood, and she dragged the crumpled sheet over her exposed limbs in an agony of mortification. 'No...' she said sickly, stricken by such cruelty.

'Yes. Six years ago I could make you burn just by looking at you——'

'That's a lie!'

'Your skin would flush, your eyes would fire and you'd shift in your seat like a cat being forced over hot coals. You wanted me then...you just wouldn't admit it,' he condemned fiercely.

Stunned, she buried her hot face in the pillow.

'At first, I didn't think of you as a tease. You were so patently unawakened. I knew you were a virgin——'

'*Stop it!*' she gasped.

'But then came that afternoon here when we only made it on to this self-same bed by a mighty feat of self-control on my part. If we hadn't been disturbed, I'd have had you,' he reminded her callously. 'After that, you were *mine.*'

'No, I wasn't!' she cried in turmoil.

'No woman, inexperienced or otherwise, responds like that to one man and then marries another a week later, still busily maintaining that she madly loves the unfortunate groom. At least, no honest, decent woman...' he gibed.

'Shut up, Carlo!' There was a sob in her voice. Initially she *had* gone to Simon, determined that their marriage should not take place. Confessing all, she had expected Simon to be outraged. Instead he had asked her if she loved Carlo. And she had uttered a vehement no. Nothing in the emotions Carlo aroused had fitted her concept of love. She had seen only lust and a terrifying self-seeking greed for pleasure in what had happened between them. She had grown up watching her mother demonstrate those same traits.

Carole had always done what she wanted, taken what she wanted, careless of the pain she caused others. And Jessica had seen the same frightening stamp on her own behaviour with Carlo. She had seen what she believed she might become without Simon to hold her steady. What Carlo had made her feel had petrified her. And Simon's love offered unconditionally had seemed a safe sanctuary. At the time she had been desperately, humbly grateful for his seeming loyalty, his pleas and assurances about needing her...and not being able to face the future without her.

Hard fingers abruptly closed round her wrist. Dully she lifted her head. Carlo wrenched off her wedding-ring and sent it skimming across the room. 'You don't need that in my bed. He wasn't very much on your mind anyway, was he, *cara*?' he breathed with an insolent smile.

'Why do you have to be so *cruel*?'

'I have a photographic memory of you walking down the aisle in your virginal white dress to marry another man!' he raked back at her.

'Well, why should that have bothered you? You didn't want to marry me!'

'That rankled, did it?' Carlo incised.

'I hated you...how could it? And I certainly had no desire to be your travelling tart!'

'*Scusi*?' He looked blank.

'Forget it,' she mumbled, but *she* never had. That day it had been the last straw when Carlo smoothly suggested she travel round the world with him.

He had said he would 'look after her'. That she could have 'anything her heart desired'. That, unfortunately, he wasn't 'into marriage or serious commitment', as he had put it.

That sadly, 'such arrangements didn't last forever', but he could promise that she would 'have a wonderful time while it did'.

And if that hadn't qualified as an offer to be a travelling tart, she didn't know what did. It had set the final seal of humiliation on their brief intimacy. Carlo hadn't loved her, hadn't cared about her...hadn't even respected her. She had just been a stupid girl from a small town very nearly conned into his bed for an hour of entertainment. And then there had been the unholy delight he had demonstrated at the idea of taking her from Simon.

She listened to him running the shower in the bathroom, endured the only slowly subsiding ache in her unsatisfied body. Well, now she knew, didn't she? She knew now that she was still every bit as vulnerable as she had feared. And Carlo had proved his point, she reflected bitterly, stiff with self-loathing. She did *want* him, probably much as a drug addict craved a fix, knowing that it was dangerous and self-destructive but unable to kill the craving. And if it was humanly possible she hated him more than ever for forcing her to concede that reality. The next three months were going to be a one-way ticket to hell. An exercise in constant humiliation.

Half an hour later, after phoning Dr Guthrie to learn that her father had spent an undisturbed night, she joined

Carlo for breakfast. As she crossed the room towards him, clad in tailored ski pants and a loose green sweater, she was furiously conscious of his critical appraisal.

'Today we go down to London and buy you a new wardrobe and a ring,' he drawled flatly. 'Thursday, we fly to the Caribbean——'

'The Caribbean?' she repeated, losing some of her carefully applied cool front. 'Is that where your father lives?'

He ignored the question. 'That gives you three days to tie up your own affairs here.'

'What about my job?' she suddenly demanded.

'You work?' Carlo elevated a brow.

'I'm a legal secretary. I'm on holiday right now because my boss is,' she conceded slowly, biting at her lower lip. 'He's not likely to give me three months' leave——'

'Tell him you've found more interesting employment.'

'You don't give a damn about me losing my job, do you?' Jessica splintered back.

Impassive dark eyes rested on her angry face. 'When this is over, you can pick yourself a new position in any one of my companies.'

His complete lack of emotion chilled her. There is no sentiment in business, he had told her. A cold, scared sensation deep down inside drove away her appetite.

'No, thanks,' Jessica said jerkily. 'I'll never be *that* desperate.'

A phone buzzed and Carlo rose fluidly upright.

She found her attention roamed after him, disobedient to her brain. He was wearing an Italian-cut grey suit that fitted him like a glove and screamed expense, sheathing long, lean thighs and squaring broad muscular shoulders. Briefly she squeezed her eyes shut, despising herself.

What was she doing? Dear heaven, what was she doing? It was as if he had conjured up the dark side of her character and it was insidiously taking her over. Her skin heated, disturbing recollections of an hour past filling her conscious mind, and so real were those images that she could *feel* the touch of his hands on her flesh, *feel* the hot, hungry onslaught of his mouth on hers. With a trembling hand she poured herself another coffee, mortified by her own lack of mental discipline. It was time she got herself back under control...but just how easy was that going to be with Carlo calling all the shots? Perspiration dampened her brow.

A manservant showed Jessica into a beautiful bedroom. He reappeared several times, laden with the day's shopping, and offered to unpack for her. Her skin warming, Jessica said thank you but no and as soon as he was gone she locked the door behind him.

Before today she had not appreciated that the purchase of clothes could be embarrassing...until Carlo took her shopping, that was. She had been trailed round, thrust in and out of every outfit which attracted him and forced to parade like a concubine for his appraisal in the kind of revealing clothes she would never have chosen for herself.

The ring on her engagement finger was a stunningly noticeable diamond cluster that literally weighed down her hand. She also had diamond earrings and a slender gold watch that had undoubtedly cost thousands, although nothing as indiscreet as price had been mentioned in Cartier within her hearing.

'What about an ankle chain?' she had said, meaning to be sarcastic.

But Carlo had found that idea a distinct turn-on. For a split-second his businesslike detachment had evaporated. Heated golden eyes had scanned her assessingly, a sensual curve tinging his expressive mouth. 'I believe I'll shop for that item on my own,' he had murmured in a black velvet purr of anticipation.

You really couldn't afford to be sarcastic with Carlo.

'We'll dine out tonight,' he had decreed after the limousine had dropped them off at his London apartment.

An hour and a half later, she regarded her reflection in the mirror with scorn. The sapphire-blue cocktail dress lovingly defined every breath she drew, never mind her body. It was the kind of dress which screamed 'I want to be noticed,' and Jessica had never suffered from such a need.

But you're playing a part, she reminded herself doggedly, surveying the ring with a curled lip. And maybe if she could prove to Carlo that she could play that part well, he would be less keen to force her into bed. A subconscious voice told her she was tilting at windmills but Jessica did not easily accept defeat.

Nor did Carlo. Involuntarily she recalled the sheer bloody-minded ferocity of his pursuit six years ago.

He had insisted on driving her home personally from the clinic the next day. He had already alerted her parents without her knowledge. Her father had greeted Carlo as though he had snatched his beloved daughter from the jaws of death and her mother's usual expression of boredom had evaporated the same second she saw Carlo.

He had stayed for dinner. He had talked business with her father and, when her mother had made some fleeting reference to the wedding, Carlo had smiled. 'Jessica's too young for marriage——'

'Far too young,' Carole had chipped in, making no secret of the fact that she had little time for Simon Turner.

Later, her mother had come to her room. 'Well, well, well,' she had said mockingly. 'So you've found yourself a millionaire.'

'I haven't found myself anything!' Jessica had dismissed with distaste.

'Sometimes I think I must have been handed the wrong baby at the hospital.' Carole Amory had grimaced. 'What's the matter with you?'

'Nothing. I just don't like him.'

'What a shame. I've invited him to join the rest of our guests next weekend.'

'*Mother*!'

'He's loaded, darling. He might just decide to invest in Amory's if we play our cards right. So be nice to him for your Daddy's sake. It was pretty obvious to me that the only thing Carlo Saracini is really interested in is you.'

Flowers had arrived for her every day the following week, each card adorned only with a slashed initial 'C'. Then he had phoned and asked her out to dinner. She had refused and he had laughed. The following evening she had found herself smiling glacially across a table at him, with her parents seated on either side as Carlo returned their hospitality at the Deangate.

With spectacular speed and efficiency, not to mention breathtaking effrontery, Carlo had broken into their lives, offering her father business contacts and advice, flattering the older man with his interest. Her mother had raged at her when she'd attempted to persuade her father that Carlo Saracini was not a man he wanted to know.

'If the firm goes into receivership, it'll be your fault!' Carole had told Jessica furiously. 'Carlo could help us... but he's not going to help if you offend him!'

Jessica had been shaken to appreciate that the family firm was on such rocky foundations. And the idea that Carlo Saracini had the power to make or break Amory's had horrified her. She hadn't trusted him an inch but her continuing attempts to warn off her father had fallen on deaf ears.

'He knows four times as much as I knew at the same age,' Gerald Amory had said admiringly. 'And he's

already put me in touch with a couple of very useful
people.'

Carlo had become a regular visitor to her home. Had
she ever actually been naïve enough to believe that Carlo
might simply invest in Amory's? Yes, she had been.

'I can help your father...' Carlo had drawled softly
the night he had called when she was at home alone.
'Take off that ring and you'll find out how generous I
can be.'

'I'm not for sale, Mr Saracini, and my engagement to
Simon is not some bargaining counter in a sordid deal,'
she flashed back, stiff with outrage.

Carlo had anchored one powerful hand round her wrist
and yanked her up against him. 'Isn't it?' he had murmured fiercely, dark golden eyes searching her furious
face. 'You know how much I want you——'

'Because you can't have me!' she had rebutted, struggling to pull free from the disturbing proximity of his
lean, all male body. 'That's the only reason you say you
want me, isn't it? I'm not interested and your ego can't
take that lying down!'

'But you are interested,' Carlo had breathed almost
amusedly. 'Do you really think I don't know when a
woman wants me, *cara*?'

'I love Simon!' she had slung back.

'Who treats you like a little sister——'

'That's not true——'

'Then tell me when he last kissed you like *this* . . .' And
before she could forestall him, Carlo had crushed her
mouth under his and it had been like being struck by
forked lightning. Terrifying.

Jessica sank back to the present and found her fingers
shakily touching her lips. She saw more clearly now than
she had seen then. Just as Carlo had, ironically, seen
more as an outsider looking on. Carlo alone had registered the lack of sexual tension between Jessica and
Simon. But Carlo had cynically misread her behaviour.

He had believed she was using Simon as a weapon against him, using Simon and her fast approaching wedding to pressure him into offering her more. And in return, Carlo had used Amory's to balance the equation.

Lifting the phone, she rang Dr Guthrie to ask after her father and was delighted to hear that her father was still angrily insisting that he had had no thought of harming himself but that he was, none the less, greatly relieved to be told that he was no longer facing prosecution.

She joined Carlo in the lounge with a ramrod-straight back and a rigidly uncommunicative face, unaware that her amethyst eyes sparkled with all the angry turmoil she was struggling to hide.

Lean and lithe in his dinner-jacket, Carlo strolled forward, a faint flush highlighting his hard cheekbones as he scanned her with hooded eyes. 'Let your hair down. I don't like it up.'

'Tough.' Jessica tilted her chin.

It was a mistake. Carlo caught her to him with one hard hand and ruthlessly released her hair from the sleek plait she had confined it in. A mass of silver cascaded untidily to her shoulders, framing her outraged face and glittering eyes.

'You look messy now...as if you just got out of my bed,' Carlo delineated in a scorching purr of satisfaction. 'I think that's more the look we're aiming for...and *this*——' He lifted her hand and tugged off the diamond ring. 'While I appreciate your enthusiasm, I don't want to see you wearing it until we take off for the Caribbean.'

Colour surged painfully up her slender throat. 'I hate you, Carlo,' she enunciated with husky clarity.

'If you want your father off the hook, *cara*...' Carlo let the smooth words hang threateningly in the air between them. 'You really are going to have to work on your attitude.'

Jessica turned paper-white.

Carlo surveyed her with pitiless dark eyes, his powerful features hard and unyielding. 'You're useless to me if you can't act the part with conviction.'

Shattered by the sheer cruelty of that uncompromising reminder, Jessica couldn't even find her voice, but inside herself she seethed with a combustible mix of mortified pride, thwarted fury and helpless fear.

Carlo let the silence drag. He spread both hands in a fluid motion. 'Do you want to go home again?'

Jessica trembled. She wanted to slap him hard. Her feathery lashes lowered over her expressive eyes. He didn't have to humiliate her like this. He didn't have to hold her father over her as if he were flexing a whip over a wild animal. Hatred powered through her slight frame but with the greatest difficulty she held it in.

'No, I don't want to go home,' she muttered grittily.

'Good,' Carlo retorted drily.

He handed her a comb in the limousine.

'You didn't need to threaten me,' she said tightly.

'This isn't a game. I don't want any temperamental displays in my father's home. Your act has to be credible.'

But why, she wanted to demand. Why...why was such a deception necessary? It could only be for money, she decided. Carlo's father must want him to marry and, unwilling to sacrifice his freedom in the long term, Carlo was prepared to deceive in the short term. Her eyes filled with scorn and disgust.

He took her to a fashionable restaurant where their entrance attracted a discreet wave of turned heads and murmured comment. Studying the menu, Jessica was vaguely surprised to register that she was really hungry.

'Don't you think it's time you told me something about your father?' she prompted.

'Where do you want me to begin?' His clipped tone was not encouraging.

'I'm not likely to put on much of an act without *some* background information. You said that he was dying——'

'Heart disease,' Carlo filled in flatly. 'He's in a wheel-chair——'

Jessica felt suddenly very insensitive. 'Can nothing be——?'

'The last operation failed. He is not strong enough for another.'

Jessica swallowed. 'Is his wife still alive?'

Unexpectedly, Carlo laughed, but the sound was curiously sardonic. 'Very much so. Sunny is considerably younger than my father.' His handsome mouth hardened, a tiny muscle pulling tight at the corner of his lips, adding a chilling gravity to his dark features. 'She is his fourth wife.'

'His *fourth*?' she couldn't help echoing weakly. 'Do you have brothers and sisters?'

'One sister, much older than I, born of his first marriage. I did have a half-brother but he was drowned in a boating accident several years back,' Carlo proffered without emotion.

'I'm sorry.'

'Don't be. He was so much older, I barely knew him.'

Jessica was silenced. Carlo was describing an impossibly fragmented family tree quite alien to her.

'My sister, Marika, lived with my father. She has never married. They live on a tiny cay in the Turks and Caicos Islands.'

'Were you born there?'

'I was born in Greece. After my mother's death, I was sent to school in Italy.'

'Why so far away?'

'I didn't like my new stepmother any more than she liked me,' Carlo said drily.

A tall, rake-thin brunette with huge dark eyes and a ripe, sultry mouth stopped by their table. Ignoring

Jessica, she spoke to Carlo in Italian. His response, whatever it was, was not to the other woman's taste. Her cheeks flamed, her eyes widening. She sent Jessica a scorching look of loathing but her dark eyes were full of pain and jealousy before she shrugged and walked back to a table nearby.

'And who was that?' Jessica couldn't help asking.

'Nobody you need concern yourself with,' Carlo said dismissively.

Jessica could feel the brunette's eyes burning into her profile. Uncomfortable with the sensation, she concentrated on her meal.

She felt claustrophobic in the limousine.

'Who was that woman?' she heard herself ask again as they entered the apartment. Disturbingly, she found that she could think of nothing else.

'Jealous, *cara*?' Carlo cast her a mocking, slanting smile.

Her slender frame taut with disbelief, Jessica very nearly choked. '*Jealous*? Are you crazy?'

Before she could move away, Carlo linked his arms round her narrow shoulders and gazed down at her with eyes the colour of molten gold. 'You're the crazy one,' he murmured huskily. 'No woman has ever made me want her as I want you.'

Her breath snarled up in her throat. She was caught unprepared.

'Would you fight for me the way I would fight for you?' Carlo enquired in the same deep-pitched tone of intimacy. 'I should have kidnapped you six years ago...'

'S-stop it, Carlo!' Jessica relocated her voice clumsily, every bone in her body tensing under the perceived threat.

Instead, he dropped his arms to her waist, bent and swept her up off her feet. At the same instant he covered her startled lips with a dark, fierce hunger that devoured. She felt the leap of response inside her and fought it to the last ditch.

He laid her down on a bed in the moonlight. 'I don't want this, Carlo,' she protested tautly. 'It isn't enough for me.'

He slung his tie aside, shrugged fluidly out of his jacket and came down beside her. 'What would be enough?' he demanded darkly, harshly, and before she could roll away out of reach to the other side of the wide bed he brought both hands down hard on hers, imprisoning her. 'What did *he* have that I didn't? What could *he* give you that I couldn't?'

Stunned by the seething anger she had ignited, Jessica stared up at him. He was talking about Simon again. 'It wasn't like that. You couldn't understand——'

'Then bloody make me understand!' Carlo invited in raw challenge. 'Was he a better lover than I was?'

Torn by a pain she had never shared with another living soul, Jessica wrenched her head to one side, seeking to evade his glittering scrutiny. 'Carlo...'

'I want to know,' he intoned, twisting one powerful hand into her hair to force her eyes back to his. 'So you tell me, what was it about him that made him so special?'

'I'm not going to talk about this!' Tears stung her eyes in a blinding surge.

'I want to talk about it. I offered you everything I had to give and you walked away...' Carlo returned with smouldering bite. 'And yet it was *me* you wanted——'

'*No*!' she gasped.

'*Si*...' Carlo snarled down at her.

'Wanting isn't enough!' she suddenly screamed back at him.

'But without it, there's nothing,' Carlo pointed out with devastating simplicity.

And the reality of that fact was like a knife twisting inside her. A tortured sob escaped her convulsed throat. She had had a marriage that was five years of nothing.

'Don't cry...' Carlo smoothed a not quite steady hand over her damp cheek and she found herself turning into the seductive warmth of that caress like a homing pigeon.

The awareness that she could not restrain her physical impulses this close to him merely added to her torment. She was her mother's daughter, a little voice said, and a sick sense of shame stirred inside her. Carlo had eased a supportive hand beneath her shoulder blades to raise her up and her fingers accidentally brushed against his broad chest and heat sprang up beneath her fingertips, the raw heat of his flesh below the thin silk shirt.

He trembled, and for some reason that made her want to do it again. He muttered something rough into the veil of her hair and she let her hand stay where it was, listening to the ruptured rasp of his breathing and feeling the thunderous crash of his heartbeat against her palm.

The atmosphere was explosive, abruptly, inexplicably exhilarating as adrenalin surged through her veins. She let her fingers spread and flex and without warning Carlo groaned, sweeping her with a sudden current of live-wire excitement.

'*Maledizione!*' Carlo muttered thickly, dragged her lithely back down on the bed. 'With you I have less control than a teenager!'

He was shaking in the circle of her arms. When had she closed her arms round him? It didn't seem important. Briefly, crazily, she experienced an extraordinary sense of power. A heartbeat later it was torn from her by the burning assault of his hungry mouth. Her body leapt into throbbing life and rational thought ended for long, timeless minutes.

The scent of him was so achingly familiar it was an aphrodisiac. His shirt was open and she found the sleek, smooth brown skin of his shoulder with her tongue and he shuddered against her, chest to breast, thigh to thigh in a pagan feast of agonising, uncontrollable excitement. Carlo rolled over and wrenched violently at her dress. She heard something tear. It meant nothing to her.

With a ragged gasp of pleasure he bent over her bared breasts, shaping her, touching her. She closed her eyes, arched her slender throat and was lost in a world of sensory overdrive, more powerful and more primitive than anything she had ever dreamt of experiencing. Scorching heat surged through her shivering body in an unstoppable surge.

Her hands fluttered over every part of him she could reach, torn between the black silk luxuriance of his hair and the oiled smoothness of the muscles flexing on his back. She wanted to touch him everywhere at once, burned to explore him as intimately as he was exploring her.

Her nails skidded down the long sweep of his back and he moaned against her mouth, biting erotically at her lower lip in punishment. Rawly impatient hands dealt with the scrap of silk that was all that shielded her from him. When he found the damp, eager heat of her, a wild cry escaped her. She was poised like a diver on the edge of a deep, beckoning abyss and she knew she would throw herself off even though she couldn't swim. The sheer primitive need she was controlled by was closer to agony than ecstasy.

'You're *mine* ... from this moment on,' Carlo spelt out roughly, 'you are mine.'

She collided with glittering dark eyes, unreadable in the moonlight, and her mouth ran suddenly dry, a shaft of returning sanity tightening her every muscle in rejection.

But his hand slid over her quivering body, shattering her with her own response. There was a buzzing sound somewhere in the background. She closed it out but after a while Carlo began to tense. Abruptly, he lifted his dark head and swore viciously under his breath. A second later, he rolled away from her and the light went on as he answered the phone.

It took several seconds for Jessica to appreciate that Carlo was talking in fast, urgent Italian. He cast aside the phone, his starkly handsome features pale and rigidly cast, his brilliant dark eyes hooded. Without a word or a glance, he strode out of the room.

Jessica was in a passion-induced daze, only slowly fumbling her way back to the real world. But at Carlo's exit she sat up. Dear God, had he had bad news about his father? In confusion she absorbed her own nudity and, hurriedly vacating the bed, found a robe to pull on. She wanted to go to Carlo, offer sympathy and comfort, and the instant she recognised that need within her, she collapsed down on the edge of the mattress and covered her face with unsteady hands.

Dear heaven, what was happening to her? What was going on inside her head? For six years she had told herself that she hated this man and yet a mere second ago her most driving urge had been to rush to his side and ease his pain by whatever means were within her power. Suddenly, she was plunged into complete turmoil by the conflicting signals between her thoughts and her emotions. Fearfully she sought to rationalise her feelings.

So much had happened so fast, she told herself weakly. This whole situation put her under severe strain. In addition, she was deeply ashamed of the fact that she could not withstand Carlo's blatant sexuality. Really it was hardly surprising, she decided, that her emotions should become wildly confused as well. She was only now learning the kind of things that most women already knew by their late teens. Desire was not love but maybe her puritanical inner self wanted her to behave as though it were. Was that what was the matter with her?

She didn't know how long she had been sitting there when she glanced up and saw Carlo framed in the doorway. He was still and silent as a statue.

Jessica swallowed hard, intimidated by his aggressive stance. 'What's wrong?'

Carlo released his breath with an audible hiss. 'Why didn't you tell me that your father was in a nursing home?' he demanded.

'How did you find out?' Sharply disconcerted, Jessica stared at him wide-eyed.

'My PA, Spiros, attempted to contact him this evening. He called to let me know and I have just finished speaking to Dr Guthrie on the phone.'

Jessica lost every scrap of colour.

'Why didn't you tell me?' Carlo thundered with sudden raw condemnation. 'Why didn't you tell me that he was in an unstable frame of mind?'

Jessica rose unsteadily upright, shattered by his fury. 'I didn't think——'

'What didn't you think? That it would make any difference to me?' Carlo's outrage was so great, he could barely vocalise the question. Strain had etched lines into his sun-bronzed skin, flattened his sensual mouth. 'Is this your opinion of me? That I would happily drive a man to suicide?'

Jessica trembled. Voiced like that, it sounded appalling. 'I only thought you wouldn't consider it . . . relevant——'

'Relevant.' Carlo only got the repetition out with the greatest of visible difficulty, his accent scissoring along the syllables like a cut-throat razor.

'My father insists that he was not trying to harm himself,' she heard herself protesting weakly. Carlo was looking at her as if he had never seen her before. And it was equally obvious that he did not like what he did see.

'Last night you made no attempt to tell me that your father was in such extreme distress . . . not once did you even hint of such a danger!' he spelt out with sizzling disbelief.

'I didn't think you'd care.'

Carlo went white and spun away from her, both hands clenched into fists. 'I don't think I have ever been closer to physical violence than I am now,' he bit out in seething incredulity. 'How dare you say to me that I would not have cared? *Dio* ... to think I almost made love to you! What did I ever do that you should view me in such a light?'

Jessica bent her head, attacked by sudden shame and confusion. Carlo was so absolutely appalled by what he had learnt. 'I ... I——'

'Had I known of your father's state of mind, I would have done everything within my power to reduce his distress. *Everything*,' he stressed, surveying her with scorching intensity. 'Did you really believe that my desire for you would outweigh the worth of a man's life? Or even the smallest risk of him taking that life?'

'No, I didn't ...' Jessica was shaking.

Carlo's golden eyes raked her with derision. 'Or were you just looking for a damned good excuse to come back to me without sacrificing your precious pride?'

She flinched as though she had been struck but she was in no condition to respond. When *had* she turned Carlo into the very image of vicious corruption inside her own head? When and on what grounds had she shorn him of every decent human emotion? Dear God, why had she deceived herself that way? For she had deceived herself. She saw that now. Had it been easier to blacken Carlo and blame him for everything sooner than face the extent of her own culpability? And worst of all, had she done that purely to avoid coming to terms with what Carlo made her feel?

'You said that there was no sentiment in business,' she attempted desperately to defend herself. 'You said that you had no interest in my father except as a means to an end and that the subject bored you.'

Reminded of those harsh words, Carlo swung away from her. 'I had no idea of your father's depression, no knowledge of your parents' divorce or of your mother's death,' he muttered less aggressively.

Jessica couldn't think straight. She felt sick inside. She saw quite clearly that last night at the Deangate she should instantly have told Carlo what had happened to her father. Yet she had not even considered telling him. She had been so punch-drunk on her image of Carlo as a sadist that she had remained silent.

'I should have told you,' she heard herself whisper.

Carlo wasn't even listening. 'I will meet with your father tomorrow and set his mind at rest. I will not have him on my conscience,' he asserted, shooting her a glance of smouldering condemnation. 'And to further that end I will tell him that I have offered you a job as my secretary.'

'That's what I intended to——'

'Believe me,' Carlo cut in fiercely, 'had I known yesterday what I know now, I would never have touched you! Just to think of you lying in my bed smugly thinking that you were sacrificing yourself for your father's life...' His teeth gritted and he spread his hands in violent rejection of the idea, his dark features pale and taut. 'That disgusts me, but it also makes me want to shake you until your teeth rattle!'

'Don't you dare!' Jessica gasped.

Carlo reached out a punitive hand and hauled her up against him without warning, his sheer strength intimidating her. Flaming golden eyes clashed with hers and she stopped breathing. 'You're not a martyr, *cara* ... you're a coward!' he seethed down at her with lancing derision. 'You want me every bit as much as I want you but you haven't got the guts to admit it!'

'Let go of me!' Jessica suddenly sobbed in turmoil.

Carlo released her so abruptly, she fell back against the bed. Spinning on his heel, he strode out of the room.

Picking herself up, Jessica slammed the door after him and then she leant back against it, tears streaming down her convulsed face, trapped in a morass of pain and emotional turmoil. She understood the turmoil but she didn't understand the pain. She could not explain to herself why it should hurt so much when Carlo looked at her with distaste and derision.

CHAPTER FIVE

'...A TREMENDOUS opportunity for me,' Gerald Amory continued with satisfaction. 'A challenge is exactly what I need right now, and I've always liked Scotland.'

Jessica gave her excited father a strained smile. Carlo had offered him the management of an ailing engineering company in Glasgow. And her father, seemingly a broken man mere days ago, had been so boosted by Carlo's apparent faith in his abilities that he was a changed personality. There was a new spring in his step and a look of energy in his tautened features that she hadn't seen in a very long time.

'He couldn't have been more understanding,' Gerald murmured, not for the first time. 'But obviously I couldn't let him write off the money I took from Amory's.'

Jessica gave him a look of shock. 'Carlo suggested that?'

'Yes, but I couldn't let him do it. I have some very valuable antiques in this house and I intend to clear the lot. I want to start with a clean sheet. I should have done it years ago. I should never have stayed in this house with all its memories of your mother,' he said with a wry grimace. 'Nor should I have agreed to stay on at Amory's, not when I felt like a dog in the manger. That was taking the easy way out. I should have restructured my life then and moved on just as your mother did. I expect to be free of my debt to Carlo within two years and who knows, with a little belt tightening, maybe sooner!'

This was said with such good cheer that Jessica simply stared, but she was inwardly digesting the astonishing news that Carlo had tried to persuade him that there was no necessity for him to return the money he had stolen.

'As for Amory's and my abrupt departure...' Gerald sighed. 'Everybody thought I had been suddenly taken ill and that's why I was rushed out of the building. Of course my secretary and the chief accountant know the truth but neither of them will talk. I've been very fortunate, although I'm not quite as slow on the uptake as you and Carlo seem to imagine, Jess...'

In receipt of his suggestive smile, Jessica said, 'Meaning?'

'Even when I finally managed to convince Carlo that yes, I had reached a very low ebb but no, I did not intend to put an end to my existence,' Gerald Amory asserted squarely, 'Carlo was still set on being extraordinarily generous. And I can think of only one reason for that.'

Jessica sat very taut.

'He has to be in love with you.'

Jessica forced a laugh. 'He offered me a job, Dad. That's all!'

Her father shook his head with a rueful smile. 'You're a very junior employee at Fulton and Greenbury and he's a tycoon. You don't even know how to use a computer, Jess. I don't think he's shipping you out to the Caribbean to stay with his family for your secretarial skills alone. At least, if he is, he's in for a very frustrating time of it!'

Jessica didn't know what to say but her father didn't seem to expect any response. He was an astute man and she should have known he would pick holes in so thin a cover story. Carlo in love with her? She couldn't even summon up any amusement at the idea. She hadn't seen or heard from Carlo since that night, three days earlier.

He had been gone when she breakfasted the next morning and she had been driven home to the cottage.

Spiros, Carlo's PA, had phoned her yesterday to tell her when she would be picked up to be taken to the airport tomorrow. He had also dropped the news that Carlo would only be meeting up with them in Miami for the final leg of the journey.

Now, as her father took his leave, eager to embark on the challenges ahead of him, Jessica was left to cope with her own confusion. Astonishingly, Carlo had gone to great lengths to help her father without hurting his pride. He had been far more generous than she could ever have expected. She had grossly underestimated Carlo. But then, she reflected ruefully, Carlo had not displayed an honourable or more appealing side to his character six years ago. Carlo had been ruthless, arrogant and aggressive. Feeling threatened, she had clung all the harder to her belief that she loved Simon.

She had loved Simon for a good half of her life and had been too inhibited by her mother's promiscuous example to question Simon's lack of sexual interest in her before their marriage. She had been grateful for his restraint, for what she had seen as his *respect* for her. For the first time she openly acknowledged that Simon had cruelly betrayed her trust.

He should have told her the truth. He shouldn't have pretended. He had had no right to use her simply to silence his family's suspicions, plunging them both into deep unhappiness and endless pretences. Why had she blamed Carlo for the misery of her marriage? she now asked herself. The reality was that her marriage would have been a disaster even if she had never met Carlo... only, having met Carlo and confessed all to Simon, she had given Simon an excuse to hide behind. Simon had allowed her to believe that her moral lapse with Carlo was what kept him from her bed. It had been a very long time before he'd admitted the truth.

And in the interim of tortured guilt she had hated Carlo and kept on hating him with quite irrational fervour. Carlo had become the focus for her bitter dissatisfaction with her life. But common sense told her that she could never have been that attracted to a man she truly hated. No, what she had really hated was the uncontrollable chemistry she experienced in Carlo's radius, a powerful sexual attraction that she couldn't handle and was deeply ashamed of feeling.

So where did that leave her now? She had scarcely slept the last few nights. She couldn't get Carlo out of her mind and that, frankly, terrified her.

Jessica boarded the luxurious jet at Miami and surveyed her superbly comfortable surroundings with a faint frown line between her brows. 'Nothing like travelling in style.'

Spiros laughed. 'Mr Philippides likes his guests to be comfortable.'

'Who is Mr Philippides?' Jessica enquired of the likeable young Greek, who had unbent from his strict formality with every hour of the travel they had shared.

Spiros sent her an incredulous glance. 'You are joking, yes?'

'Why should I be joking?' Jessica dropped into her seat and wondered when Carlo intended to show. Her nervous tension was heightening by the second.

Spiros frowned and leant forward. 'Lukas Philippides is Carlo's father, Miss Amory,' he proffered awkwardly. 'Of course, you knew . . . you are pulling my foot——'

'Leg,' Jessica corrected, frozen to stillness by shock.

Spiros chuckled. 'Who has not heard of Lukas Philippides?'

'Who indeed?' she mumbled through a dry mouth. Lukas Philippides was one of the richest men in the world and in recent years he had lived like a recluse, encouraging the media to concoct wildly unlikely stories about him and compare him to the late Howard Hughes.

Spiros was studying her closely. 'You really didn't know,' he realised with unhidden astonishment. 'But the relationship is widely known. Carlo dropped the Philippides name and took his mother's many years ago.'

Damn Carlo for his refusal to fill her in on the most basic facts! That was her first thought. Her standing as his supposed fiancée might very easily have fallen at the first ditch had she betrayed her ignorance in the wrong company. Lukas Philippides was dying and the media had yet to stumble on that scoop. All that money, an amount of money beyond her comprehension, was shortly to be up for grabs. Carlo had been playing for far higher stakes than she could ever have imagined, she thought sickly. Wealth beyond avarice, the kind of inheritance many would kill for... never mind lie and deceive.

Jessica was badly shaken. Carlo's fury that she had failed to tell him of her father's depression, his astonishing kindness towards her father from that point... both those things had demonstrated a new side to Carlo's volatile nature. But now she found her most recent assumptions being flung into chaos all over again.

Had Lukas Philippides demanded that his son marry before he could inherit? She could think of no other reason for Carlo's deception. And how likely was it that a man like Lukas Philippides would find a twenty-six-year-old widow without any assets an acceptable match for his only surviving son and heir? The plot thickens, she thought hysterically. What the hell had she got herself into?

The stewardess was speaking. Jessica lifted her head as Carlo appeared. He dropped down with fluid energy into the seat opposite her. His impact was incredibly physical. In a lightweight, exquisitely cut cream suit that threw his exotic darkness into prominence, he was shatteringly sleek and beautiful in an entirely masculine way. Undoubtedly not a single female head had failed to turn on his passage here. This proximity to Carlo was like being struck by lightning.

Her body reacted involuntarily to the powerful sexuality he emanated. Beneath her silk camisole she could feel her nipples tighten into hard little points and a quiver ran through her as she attempted to remove her eyes from the magnetic gold allure of his. Her heartbeat thudded in her eardrums and it was suddenly impossible to breathe in the rushing silence.

'You missed me,' Carlo positively purred, stretching out his long, lean thighs in an attitude of indolent relaxation as the jet engines whined up to take-off. He rested his dark head back and surveyed her from below a screen of lush black lashes, hooding his gaze to a sliver of gleaming awareness. 'I can feel the heat from here.'

A hectic flush coloured her cheekbones. Her soft mouth tightened. She felt entrapped by her own weakness, as easily read as a pre-teen suffering from a giant crush. Carlo let his eyes wander with sensual intensity over her, his attention lingering shamelessly on the taut buds of her tilted breasts plainly visible beneath her camisole. She threw up her chin. 'It's the air-conditioning!' she snapped in outrage.

Carlo was still laughing when they were airborne. He twisted his head and said something to Spiros, who was seated behind him. The younger man left his seat as the stewardess appeared with a tray of drinks and her attention was so entirely pinned to Carlo that she very nearly spilt Jessica's.

But she might as well not have existed. Carlo's attention was centred with smouldering potency on Jessica. Releasing his belt, he slid upright and settled down beside her. Removing her drink from her nerveless fingers, he pulled her out of her seat with easy strength and yanked her down on top of him. He took her by surprise, and she collapsed across his hard thighs in a tangle of limbs.

'What the hell——?'

Both lean hands pinned to her cheekbones, he drove his tongue deep into her mouth in a hot, erotic invasion that sent her every sense into instant, shuddering meltdown. With a husky groan, he repeated the assault in a blatant imitation of a far more intimate possession and a tight, coiled spring of need fired her every skin cell. She couldn't get enough of him. He was a feast after a famine, the heat of the tropics after a long, endless winter and she was helplessly greedy for every sensation so long denied.

'There's a very comfortable bed in the cabin.' His palms still framing her face, brilliant golden eyes, blazing with desire, scanned hers.

Simultaneously, her nostrils flared. Obsession. A definable aroma of the exclusive perfume clung to him. Her stomach twisted painfully. Carlo had been in close bodily contact with another woman. Nausea doused her excitement. She jerked her head free and slid upright on wobbly legs.

'No doubt you're very familiar with those kinds of facilities.'

An ebony brow elevated. 'Do you want the truth or a polite fiction? Of course there have been women in my life, but never more than one at a time.'

Furiously she turned her head away. All she could smell was that perfume and it was turning her stomach now, reminding her what a fool she was in this male's presence. He made her wanton, reckless. It was one thing to acknowledge his attraction, another thing entirely to accept that that same attraction could humiliate her. Her lips still stung from the carnal imprint of his, her unsatisfied body still ached. But she was torturingly certain that Carlo was not suffering from similar rigours of celibacy. Carlo had been with another woman...and why not?

This was the son of one of the twentieth century's most renowned womanisers. Four wives and innumerable mistresses. And six years ago Carlo had acted like a real chip off the old block, offering her nothing

but sex and the good life and the cool assurance that
marriage wouldn't feature anywhere in the equation.
Perhaps it was time she reminded herself that all Carlo
was doing now was putting a sensual gloss on their supposed relationship for his father's benefit.

'What do you want from me?'

The answer came inwardly. Much more than you will
give... It shook her.

'Together we're sexual dynamite. Why deny yourself
the pleasure I can give you?' Grimly amused dark eyes
rested assessingly on her taut profile and unexpectedly
she turned and caught the gleam of mockery.

'You didn't expect me to go into that cabin with
you... did you?'

'I like watching you torment yourself,' Carlo confided, the full intensity of his probing gaze resting on
her. 'You're a fascinatingly complex little creature.
Passionate and repressed. Wild and inhibited. And secretive, intensely secretive...'

Her lips compressed bloodlessly. 'I don't know what
you mean.'

Carlo laced lean brown fingers calmly round his glass
and surveyed her as if she were a specimen under a
microscope. 'What made you what you are? What goes
on inside that beautiful head? Most of my women have
told me the story of their lives by the end of the second
date. But you tell me nothing and you never did. Not
about your family, not about your marriage. You keep
it all locked up tight inside...'

'I am not one of your women, Carlo.' But it was a
shaken retort. She was appalled by the direction of the
conversation. It was an attack on the privacy she
cherished.

'If it were not for your father, I wouldn't even know
how your late husband died.' Carlo seemed to be selecting his words with immense care. 'I find it surpass-
ingly strange that this great love that encompassed so

many years of your life should never, ever be mentioned even accidentally. But I've yet to hear his name pass your lips.'

She stared at him with huge amethyst eyes dark with pain. 'I don't want to talk about it——'

'But isn't that unnatural? He's only been dead a year and I understand that you nursed him for many months beforehand,' Carlo continued with merciless persistence. 'Leukaemia...that must have been a harrowing experience...'

Jerkily, Jessica swung away from him. She wanted him to shut up. She wanted to cover her ears. She wanted to run away but there was no place to go. Carlo had chosen to stage his interrogation well. She folded her arms. 'It's none of your business.'

'But I've made it my business,' Carlo pointed out gently. 'By the time we part, all of my questions will have been satisfied. I will know everything about you.'

It was a threat. In defiance of her own inner insecurity, she thrust up her chin. 'And do you plan to be similarly expansive?'

'I doubt it. I tend to keep my own counsel.'

She flung her head back, silver hair flying back from her exquisite face. 'Even to the ridiculous extent of not telling me *who* your father is?'

'So the penny finally dropped.' Carlo's expressive mouth curved into a sardonic smile.

'Spiros told me and I'd like to know why you didn't!'

'It's not an announcement I've had to make in recent years. It is of no importance,' he asserted.

And suddenly she understood and she was speared by a sharp pang of pain. 'You didn't trust me, did you?' she condemned shakily. 'You knew I didn't know and you didn't trust me enough to tell me!'

A broad shoulder lifted in a fluid shrug. He met her distressed gaze unflinchingly. 'It did cross my mind that you could sell the information for hundreds of thousands of pounds in the right quarter. His death will create havoc on the international money market. Foreknowledge would give certain speculators the opportunity to make a fortune. And even if you had simply chosen to approach a tabloid, you could still have made more than sufficient money to clear your father's obligations to me.'

Jessica looked at him, incredulous and deeply wounded. 'And you think that I would have done that?'

'Let us say that I saw no reason to take an unnecessary risk.'

Numbly she shook her head. 'Dear God, what sort of woman do you think I am?'

'Tough. Been there, done that,' he traded with dry mockery. 'Delicate wrapping round a steel backbone.'

'I would never have done something so disgusting!' Jessica told him vehemently. 'I do have some standards.'

Golden eyes glittered over her tautened figure. 'Then where were they six years ago, *cara*?'

Her stomach turned over, every muscle tightening as though to ward off a punch. 'I made a mistake...a dreadful, inexcusable mistake——'

Carlo vented a sardonic laugh and drained his glass, the hard planes of his dark features chillingly set. 'Are you calling me a mistake...or *him*?' he drawled softly.

Although she was trembling, she stood her ground. 'What do you think?'

'That I will never forgive you either way.'

Sharply disconcerted, she collided with gleaming gold and it was like ice sliding slowly down her tautened spinal cord, the most frightening chill spreading with sick certainty through her limbs. The colour drained from her face.

'You're telling yourself right now that you don't want or need my forgiveness,' Carlo murmured with shattering accuracy. 'But you will find that you do. You already look for me when I'm not there, don't you, *cara*?

How did you sleep the last few nights? Did you expect me to call and wonder why I didn't? And just how did you feel when you first saw me today...elated? Sexually excited? You're halfway to falling in love with me already. I recognise all the symptoms and this is where I normally beat a strategic retreat in an affair...but not with you.'

Throughout she had stood there, entrapped by the wicked allure of his beautiful eyes and the hypnotic mastery of his rich, dark voice. She was transfixed by fascination, had to struggle just to unglue her tongue from the roof of her dry mouth. 'You're out of your mind,' she whispered. 'I could never love you.'

'I will settle for nothing less,' Carlo told her softly in the steadily thickening atmosphere.

'You belong in a cave, Carlo!' Jessica managed a laugh that sounded oddly forced even to her own ears. 'Do you honestly imagine that I have so little control over my own emotions?'

Carlo dealt her an insolent smile that made her palms itch to slap him hard. 'I hate to be crude but you have very little control over your body——'

Fury seized hold of her and she snatched up her glass and flicked the contents over him.

'And even less over your temper.' He withdrew a silk handkerchief and calmly wiped the drops from his cheekbones. 'In fact you are quite appallingly juvenile in your reactions when you do lose your head. Like a child hitting out blindly in a tantrum,' he mused reflectively. 'Almost as though you haven't allowed yourself the luxury of freely letting go of your anger very often...so you really can't handle it, can you?'

The insight inherent in that careless stab dismayed her and she stepped hurriedly back from him. 'Has the game-playing moved into the field of therapy now?' she asked with sarcasm dripping from every syllable.

'One,' Carlo itemised, 'this is not a game for me. And two, I'm more into shock treatment than therapy. I lack the necessary patience. When I want something, I want it yesterday.'

Frustration currented through her. She needed to fight back but was now too afraid that in anger she might be guilty of revealing too much. Disturbingly, Carlo smiled, his cool composure untouched. 'You should go and lie down for a while. I'll wake you up before we land on Grand Turk.'

'I don't want to lie down.' Every fibre rebelled from the concept of retreat. 'Is Grand Turk where your father lives?'

'He lives on Paradiso Cay which he owns.'

With determination, Jessica took a seat again. If she talked, she would not be required to think about Carlo's unashamed lust for revenge. 'And how long has he lived there?'

'Five years. He bought Paradiso when ill-health became a feature of his life,' Carlo said unemotionally.

'You are so filled with compassion.'

'He is not a man who inspires compassion,' Carlo fielded drily. 'And he would be furious if he was given it. He has lived his life exactly as he wanted to live it. He has never followed medical advice. He smokes, he drinks, he loves the richest of foods and his sexual appetite was once legendary. He would tell you that childhood deprivation made him greedy for the luxuries but the reality is that Lukas has never seen the need for temperance in any field and never, to my knowledge, considered any human being's needs above his own——'

Jessica swallowed hard. 'You're describing a monster, Carlo.'

Quite spontaneously, Carlo laughed. 'To you, perhaps, for restraint in all things is your holy icon, isn't it? Everything neat and tidy, nothing unpredictable...'

She dredged her startled gaze from him. 'You were talking about your father——'

'He's volatile, fiercely proud, and no doubt bitterly resents his failing strength. He will fight for life to the very last moment and will probably die cursing all who survive him.'

'Does that include you?'

'I would hope not.' Carlo's strong features shadowed and then he shrugged with Latin acceptance. 'But I would not like to make a career out of second-guessing Lukas. He loves surprising people. A pussycat one moment, a predator the next——'

'A lot like you, then,' she muttered in a 'forewarned is forearmed' tone.

'At least what you see is what you get with me.'

But what did she see? she questioned, flipping her vulnerable eyes away out of his probing reach. So kind to her father, so unrelentingly cruel to her. He had waited until they were airborne before he told her what he had in store for her. But he couldn't make her love him. Liking and respect and sharing were the prelude to loving. 'Everything neat and tidy, nothing unpredictable...' Her teeth gritted. She wanted to tear his honey-smooth drawl out of her head, no matter how much it hurt!

How could he have thought that she might sell the revelation that his father was dying to the highest bidder? She shuddered with revulsion. Of course, she had been hurt. Nobody could easily accept such a charge. So, he didn't trust her as far as he could throw her... but what had made *him* like that? She remembered him saying that knowledge was a weapon in a woman's hands and that had come straight from the gut! Clearly at some stage Carlo had got badly burned by a member of her sex and the memory rankled, kept him on his guard, made him cynical and suspicious... so, who's playing the therapy game now, Jess?

Why was she allowing him to wind her up like this? What did any of this matter to her? All that lay between her and Carlo was sex. A demeaning passion on her side, lust on his. Though maybe lust was too strong a word. Evidently, Carlo was more powered by a desire for revenge than by his sex drive. Sex was simply the channel through which he planned to trap her. Did he really think he could make her fall in love with him?

Dear heaven, all that intellectual wheeling and dealing seemed to fail him when it came to human emotions, and to actually have the supreme self-assurance to forewarn her of his expectations...! Jessica smothered a laugh and then her nostrils flared with renewed distaste.

'You stink of perfume, Carlo. I think you should have a shower.' The suggestion simply leapt right off her tongue and it was hard to say which of them was most taken aback by it.

'*Scusi*?' Carlo lapsed into Italian, surveying her with cool enquiry.

Jessica wrinkled her nose. 'It's tacky, like lipstick on your collar.'

'What the hell are you talking about?'

'The lady left her signature, *caro*,' she dropped with dulcet sweetness. 'Her perfume. It's all over you.'

Carlo's eyes splintered into hers, alight with disturbing mockery. A slumbrous smile of staggering charisma glued her gaze to him. 'What a wonderful private eye you would make...I can see you sheltering from the rain in a doorway, watching out for the evidence of some poor bastard cheating on his wife! Unhappily for you, Jessica I am not a married man——'

'I haven't the slightest desire to know what you were doing last night!' she vented in disgust.

'It can't have been last night,' Carlo drawled. 'I had a shower this morning.'

Jessica flew upright, infuriated by his mockery. 'Do you really think I gave a damn when or with whom?'

Carlo stretched out with positive indolence, his eyes a mere glimmer of light below the luxuriant veil of his ridiculously long lashes. 'One of my PAs from the New York office. Five foot ten inches tall, Titian hair... my besetting sin,' he confided softly, reflectively, his eloquent mouth taking on a sensual slant. 'She was as wild and hot as I was. I got laid in my coffee break——'

Frozen by appalled disbelief that he could actually be confessing to such behaviour, Jessica was welded to the spot. Her vocal cords were strangled.

'And at lunchtime. She was *insatiable*,' Carlo savoured. 'Sadly the lift on the way up to my suite was occupied... that's always been one of my fantasies, but unless I close off and empty some building it looks like going unfulfilled. I'm not into audience participation. Still, we made the best of the floor, the bed, the bath, the walls, the kitchen table... and then she called up a friend and that is *really* when the fun got started...you're lucky I made the flight...'

Functioning on automatic pilot, Jessica backed away. She felt butchered. He might as well have been wielding a knife without giving her an anaesthetic. She was in agony and scared of throwing up in front of him.

'You don't want to hear about the truly perverted things we did?' Carlo raised an ebony brow in apparent surprise and then sighed. 'Good, I'm afraid my imagination is fast running out of fuel. Here... catch!'

A gift-wrapped box landed at her feet but she barely saw it before she was forced to whirl into the washroom and lose her lunch in the most humiliating fashion possible. She heard Carlo mutter a startled imprecation in her wake and wished she had had time to close the door. Just about the last thing she expected from him was help. But Carlo took over, pressing a cold cloth to her perspiring brow and offering her a glass of water to rinse out her mouth. Then he swept up her still shivering and weak body, kicked open a door and laid her down on a bed.

Her eyes skidded over him, haunted, bruised.

'*Madre di Dio!*' he launched down at her with a groan. 'It was a joke!'

She shut her eyes, too shattered to comprehend and then abruptly she rolled over, curling into a defensive foetal position as far away from him as she could get.

'It never happened! You think I'm some sort of pervert?' Carlo grated in frustration. 'I made it up... all of it! I was joking! I gave you what you seemed to expect. I do have a red-headed Amazon on my staff but she happens to be built like a tank and the happily married mother of four kids. I will never, ever buy you perfume again...'

Her nose wrinkled to force back the flood of tears threatening. The aftermath of shock, but she would sooner have been boiled alive than cry in front of him. 'If you were hanging off the edge of a cliff, I'd stand on your fingers,' she told him jerkily.

She heard paper tearing. A bottle of Obsession landed beside her.

'The name caught my eye,' he raked down at her, 'and the stupid bitch behind the counter sprayed some of it round me. That was yesterday and I still can't get rid of it!'

A long silence stretched. Her teeth bit into the hand she had wedged against her mouth but she couldn't stop the faint tremors still racking through her.

'I am sorry.' He sounded frustrated, furious and out of his depth. 'I didn't intend to upset you.'

Pull the other one, she thought bitterly, forcing herself to face head-on the extent of her self-betrayal. He tells you he's been with another woman and you go to pieces and start throwing up. Anguish trammelled through her afresh.

'There has been no woman in my bed for many weeks. Is that what you want to hear?'

No, what she really wanted to hear, she registered in agony, was that there had been no other woman in *six years*. Carlo had concentrated her mind wonderfully. She didn't have any secrets from herself now. No secret and no proud pretence could survive after what he had just put her through. She could not bear to think of him with another woman . . . all these years had not once permitted herself to envisage that reality, had not even dreamt that that reality could be so tormentingly painful to her.

Deep down inside her subconscious, Carlo had been *hers* alone. And until now she had never even known that that crazy belief existed inside her. But now the horrendous possessiveness she had discovered twisted like a knife in an open wound. She had no right to feel possessive about Carlo, no excuse to be torn apart by the most bitter and violent jealousy.

Beside her the mattress gave. 'What are you thinking?' Carlo demanded.

'Bastard!' she gasped helplessly.

'Was Turner unfaithful?'

One and one make two. Two and two make four. Carlo was already acting on signals received and computing possibilities like a champion downhill skier racing triumphantly for the finishing line. She couldn't even be bothered going through the motions of attempting to throw him off the scent. 'No,' she said wearily.

But she had grown up in the shadow of constant infidelity. Her mother had been quite unashamed of her promiscuity. Sexual freedom had been a destructive drug she was hooked on, and the older Jessica got, the more blatantly Carole had flaunted her beliefs and her men.

Jessica had found that even more deeply offensive than the screaming fits of abuse her father had regularly withstood. Forced to live in the turmoil of her parents' deeply destructive marriage, she had also been forced to stand silent and blind on the sidelines, neither commenting nor taking sides. Perhaps that was when she had begun to repress her own emotions.

'You wanted to know why I never talk about my family,' she said flatly. 'Well, here goes. My mother was once asked to leave the Deangate Hotel because the management suspected her of soliciting.'

'Soliciting?' Carlo repeated the term as though it was foreign to him.

'She used to pick up men in the bar and go up to their rooms. Not for money, for kicks. Sometimes she brought them home...the first time, I was ten,' Jessica confided shakily, 'I didn't know she was home. I was doing my homework in the kitchen and then I heard her laughing. I went upstairs and she was doing a strip for this guy...'

Carlo expelled his breath in a hiss. 'What did you do?'

'I ran away and told Simon. He told me not to tell.' An embittered laugh yanked painfully at her aching throat. 'I never told. I never told once. Daddy's little princess wasn't supposed to know about things like that. But God knows, everybody else knew my mother was the local tart. The boys at school used to laugh about her and ask me to do all sorts of...interesting things with them...after all, I was the daughter of a gifted amateur. Have you got a tape recorder running, Carlo? I would hate you to miss any of this——'

'Stop it,' he grated roughly, his arms tightening round her even though she was fiercely resisting his embrace.

'I never went out on a single date because I knew what would be expected of me. And I never had a female best friend. My mother was so notorious, nobody wanted their daughter to risk coming to my house, and how could I possibly be a *nice*, decent girl with a family background like that? Dad adored her...can you believe that?' Jessica muttered sickly. 'He pretended it wasn't happening and that meant that I had to pretend too...except with Simon. Am I mentioning his name enough for you, Carlo?'

'I don't want to hear it again,' he gritted out tautly, running a hand down her rigid back. 'Stop treating me like a leper! Why didn't your father divorce her?'

'He loved her.'

'That isn't love, it's masochism——'

'She didn't want a divorce until you bought the firm,' Jessica whispered grimly. 'There was finally enough cash to finance her escape in style. She walked out a week later and took Dad for just about all of it. I think he thought she'd go off on a spree and then come back...but she never came back...never so much as looked back——'

'And that hurt?'

'Yes.' For the very first time, she admitted to herself that it had. Even though her mother had never shown her affection, Carole's departure and years of silence had rammed the message of her disinterest home harder than anything else had. And it had hurt, but Jessica had buried that hurt.

'Go to sleep,' Carlo urged huskily.

Utterly drained, her mind floating free behind her heavy eyelids, she let her body relax into the sheltering heat of him and she slept.

CHAPTER SIX

JESSICA woke up with a start, a groan of remembered embarrassment escaping her as she sat up. She had felt half-dead when Carlo had all but carried her on to the helicopter. She had been wishing she were dead by the time she was hauled off it again, sick and in a state of collapse. Her impressions had been fleeting.

She recalled the cluster of security men converging on the helipad, blurred glimpses of an incredibly large white villa and heat that only increased the non-stop pounding behind her temples. Jet lag had finally caught up with her. A rueful grimace slanted her face as she gingerly slid out of bed to gratefully appreciate that the ground beneath her feet was no longer rocking. It was dark outside. Locating the bedside light, she glanced at her watch. Eight in the evening.

The housekeeper—at least she assumed the warm, matronly woman who had come to her assistance was the housekeeper—had been a merciful saviour. She had taken charge, banishing Carlo and helping Jessica into bed. Nor had her care ended there. Oblivious to Jessica's mortified assurances that she would be all right, the older woman had still been sitting by the bed when she finally fell asleep.

But what had possessed her yesterday? Why had she told Carlo about the misery of her adolescent years? She had told Carlo things that she had not even told Simon, things that she had never shared with anyone. And at the time she had felt curiously lightened of the burden of those unpleasant recollections, almost as though she was exorcising them and finally putting them into the past where they belonged. In a weak moment she had surrendered her most private memories . . . so why didn't she feel bad about that?

She explored the huge, opulently furnished room, complete with brocaded sofas, magnificent flower arrangements and an exquisite antique escritoire with tiny drawers filled with luxury notepaper. The adjoining bathroom and dressing-room were equally impressive. Her very cases had been unpacked and her clothing hung.

Some of her tension evaporated. There were no male accoutrements anywhere to be seen. The décor was defiantly feminine. Contrary to her expectations, she was clearly not sharing a room with Carlo. That made her breathe a little easier.

She was emerging from the shower, towelling her hair, when she thought she heard someone in the bedroom. Employing the fleecy robe supplied for her use, she hurriedly donned it.

A tall woman in a figure-hugging backless gown the shade of ripe Hamburg grapes was standing by the windows. As she turned, her waist-length torrent of curling copper hair flew round her narrow white shoulders and great green eyes with the luminosity of jewels fixed on Jessica. Without doubt, she was one of the most beautiful women Jessica had ever seen.

'I'm Sunny,' she murmured, her gaze pinned to Jessica with disturbing intensity. 'Welcome to Paradiso.'

'Jessica Amory.' Jessica struggled not to feel self-conscious about her wet hair, bare feet and scrubbed face. Sunny Philippides, her hostess, no more than a handful of years her senior and as British as she was herself. Was an unannounced invasion the usual way she greeted her guests?

Sunny strolled about the room, her pale hands touching this, adjusting that before passing by Jessica to wander into the dressing-room and skim a hand through the garments visible and then walk back out again without a shade of discomfiture. 'Did Carlo buy the clothes as a prop for the masquerade?'

'I'm sorry. I don't follow.' Jessica maintained her composure but underneath her tension was heightening.

Sunny laughed and sent her a gleaming look of amusement from below her artfully darkened copper lashes. 'I *know* . . . I know it's a masquerade. How much is he paying you? If you're good, I'll double it!'

'I don't know what you're talking about,' Jessica returned drily.

'Even the walls have ears . . . is that what he told you?' Sunny drifted fluidly over to the door. 'But you don't need to keep up the act with me. After all, I am aware that you only met Carlo for the first time last week . . .'

'I've known Carlo for six years.'

Sunny stilled and turned. 'That's impossible.'

Jessica's irritation was rising steadily. 'Why is it impossible?'

'You were married and Carlo . . .' Thrown by Jessica's announcement, Sunny frowned and then elevated an imperious brow. 'Oh that's the story is it? Clever. Lukas will appreciate it. Dinner's at nine. Don't be late,' she instructed as if she was addressing an employee.

Jessica's knees sagged as the door shut. And what was all that about? Where had Sunny got her information from? How had she known that Jessica had been married? Had Carlo told them? But surely Carlo would not have told his father's wife that the engagement was a fake? Had Sunny simply been trying to trip her up?

With a furious frown of frustration, Jessica set about drying her hair and dressing, choosing a sleek gold satin and chiffon gown which she had thought was quite over the top until she saw the villa . . . and Sunny. 'How much is he paying you? If you're good, I'll double it.' The hint that Sunny and Carlo were in partnership had been clear. Jessica swallowed hard, her stomach clenching. Carlo had some explaining to do.

Carlo...who didn't want to explain anything. Was his reluctance to explain based on the reality that the truth was distinctly unsavoury? With a hiss of impatience Jessica asked herself where her wild imagination was taking her now. She was not the melodramatic type. A recollection of that stupid scene on the jet replayed and her skin heated. She didn't want to think about that. Right now there were more important things.

A dark-skinned maid escorted her along a mile of corridors, down a palatial gilded staircase and into a drawing-room. Jessica registered her first mistake as a plump woman in a black dress adorned by an opulent diamond brooch moved forward to greet her. Not the housekeeper, she guessed, her cheekbones colouring. Marika, Carlo's sister.

'How are you feeling? I was going to send a tray up to you later. I thought you would sleep for hours.' With a firm hand she drew Jessica deeper into the room. 'She looks much better, doesn't she, Carlo? Sunny, this is Jessica...'

Sunny extended a languid hand as though they had not yet met. 'Do let me see your ring,' she enthused, holding onto Jessica's fingers with a surprisingly steely grip. 'It's gorgeous. Your choice or Carlo's?'

'A shared choice,' Jessica breathed, removing her hand again, but before she could move away Sunny tucked her arm chumily into hers so that they stood side by side.

'What do we look like together?' Sunny giggled. 'She's so *small*, Carlo!'

Carlo strolled forward, dark and devastating in an off white dinner jacket. His golden eyes burned as scorchingly bright as flames, a tiny muscle pulling at the sensual line of his mouth. Jessica sensed his faint tension but his slanting smile was a masterpiece of cool.

'How do you feel, *cara*?'

Sunny's hand dropped away. With relief, Jessica moved out of reach. 'As if I never want to board a helicopter again.'

Carlo lifted her hand and pressed his mouth hotly to the sensitive skin on the inside of her wrist. As she collided breathlessly with his hooded eyes, her every nerve-ending ran riot. 'You look ravishing,' he murmured huskily.

Act one, scene one...the Latin lover, Jessica thought tautly. He drew her down onto a sofa and signalled for a drink to be brought to her and as she took her seat, she glimpsed Sunny's furious face. Jessica looked away again. Marika started talking doggedly about clothes, seating herself beside Jessica and effectively blocking her sister-in-law from view. Carlo wandered over and stood at the windows with his back to them. Seconds later, Sunny drifted over to his side.

A humming sound turned Jessica's head. A big, broadly built man seated in a wheelchair had appeared in the doorway. Lukas Philippides had thick silver hair and a deeply lined, fleshy face. He was struggling for breath but furiously waving away the uniformed male nurse beside him. Sunken dark eyes scanned the room and centred on Jessica with perceptible force.

He lifted a hand. 'Come here,' he commanded brusquely like an old-fashioned potentate.

Helplessly, Jessica sought out Carlo. He was smiling with genuine amusement. She stood up under the glare of the huge chandelier above, her head high, her shoulders back and moved forward.

'She walks like a queen, Carlo!' Lukas Philippides subjected her to a thorough top to toe assessment. 'Small. Good breasts. Quick temper,' he concluded, reading Jessica's flashing eyes with accuracy.

'Would you like to check my teeth?' Jessica enquired.

Lukas stared at her for a startled moment and then gave a great shout of appreciative laughter. 'Spirit and a sense of humour... I like that. But can you give Carlo sons?' he demanded bluntly. 'That is the most important thing.'

Carlo banded an arm to her taut spine. 'Not to me.'

'Five years of marriage and no children,' Lukas argued fiercely. 'You think about that, Carlo... send her for some tests or something and then I'll keep quiet!'

Jessica could not quite believe that this utterly revolting conversation was carrying on above her head. Carlo said something in rapid Greek and his father snapped back at him and then cast both hands in the air with an attitude of blistering contempt.

Dinner was announced.

As they left the room in the wake of Lukas, Jessica hissed at Carlo, 'I want to talk to you!'

'You want to fight, we do it in private,' he gritted down at her roughly, a dark anger seething in his flashing sidewise glance.

And what the blue blazes did he have to smoulder about?

She asked him.

'The thought of you lying under Turner for five bloody years!' he slashed back down at her with visible distaste. 'Unproductive or otherwise.'

Jessica went white.

The dining table was circular. It was a relief to find Marika seated to one side of her. She couldn't bring herself to look at Carlo again.

'Children are very important to Greek men of my father's generation,' Carlo's sister murmured with a sigh. 'It was not his intention to hurt your feelings.'

A lie if ever there was one, even if it was meant kindly. After half an hour watching Lukas Philippides in action, it was crystal-clear that he didn't give a damn what he said or how it was received. The mere fact that Jessica was female put her in an inferior position.

Sunny was different in her husband's presence. She smiled and chattered gaily, putting on a show of great friendliness towards Jessica. She ate very little but her wine glass required constant replenishment. Father and son talked in Greek. Marika made polite, rather anxious conversation, her attention frequently straying to her sister-in-law.

Jessica was sipping her coffee when it happened. With a guttural sound of fury, Lukas reached out, snatched up his wife's glass and flung it violently against the wall. Quite unconcerned, Sunny smothered a yawn with a polite hand.

'I think I'll turn in,' Sunny said as a poker-faced man-servant began to quietly pick up the broken shards of glass.

Lukas grunted something rough in Greek and lit a fat cigar, unconcerned by the shattering silence. He gave his daughter an impatient nod.

'Would you like some fresh air, Jessica?' Marika murmured brightly on cue. 'We could walk on the terrace.'

Jessica's last view of Lukas was of him choking on the cigar and wheezing, and with the best will in the world she couldn't experience much in the way of compassion.

'My father is not a sensitive man,' Marika said with careful emphasis as soon as the doors closed behind them. 'Don't let him upset you. I wish you could have witnessed his delight and satisfaction when he learnt of your engagement. My brother is thirty-three and the news was most welcome. We were beginning to fear that he would never marry.'

'How long is it since Carlo last saw your father? Carlo doesn't talk much about his family,' Jessica added hurriedly, fearful that she had made a slip.

But his sister's plump face merely looked sad and resigned. 'Over nine years. Of course, I have always kept in touch with Carlo. I would say I was going shopping and we would meet up in Miami. I am deeply attached to Carlo,' she shared with great warmth. 'Ever since he was a little boy. I was seventeen when he was born and he was the most beautiful baby...'

They strolled along the paved terrace beneath the starry night sky while Marika gave her chapter and verse on Carlo's baby years. Her pride was touching, as was her pleasure in sharing such titbits with the woman she believed to be her brother's bride-to-be. Jessica felt horribly guilty. Marika was so kind and trusting, clearly not even dreaming that there was anything strange about her brother's sudden engagement.

'What was his mother like?' she asked encouragingly.

'She was very beautiful. Then, Lukas would not have married her otherwise,' Marika chuckled, and then her smile dimmed. 'I think, for a while, he really loved Sofia, but he wanted more children and she couldn't have them. That's why he divorced her. It was a very bitter divorce. Carlo wanted to live with his mother but my father would not allow Sofia to take Carlo away——'

'Why not?'

'Carlo was his son,' sighed Marika. 'Unfortunately, Carlo was very protective of Sofia and he blamed his father for hurting her. That's when the trouble between them began. Lukas was furious...his young son, daring to condemn him. Then Lukas remarried and Sofia died. Carlo hadn't seen his mother in many months and that made him even more bitter. Eventually he was sent off to school. When he was eighteen, he took his mother's name and I have never known my father as angry as he was then. For Lukas, it was the most base insult. He is immensely proud of the Philippides name.'

But father and son had got together again nine years ago and Jessica was insatiably curious about what had occurred to upset the apple cart then. Sufficient to sever all familial ties, to employ Carlo's phraseology.

'He forgave him, though... didn't he?' Jessica fished, and then suddenly despised herself for trying to draw his sister into telling her more.

There was no mistaking Marika's tightening features. Her gentle dark eyes hardened. 'Did he? I don't think so,' she said reflectively. 'But this time, yes. My father very much wants to win his son back to his side. He is aware of how little time may be left to him. He will not admit it but he is very proud of the success Carlo has achieved without his help.'

Hail the conquering hero, the return of the prodigal to the celebration feast.

Suddenly Marika laughed and leant closer to Jessica to whisper, 'I tell you a secret. Lukas has a library of Press cuttings on Carlo but Carlo would never believe it unless he saw with his own eyes.'

Her homely face tightened and she patted the younger woman's arm. 'I am very happy that Carlo has found it possible to love again. I feared that he would never marry. A weaker man might have had his faith in women destroyed forever by such treachery but——'

What treachery? Jessica was on the brink of asking when a manservant emerged from the villa and spoke to Marika.

'Please excuse me. My father wants me.'

'I think I'll go to bed,' Jessica said, but as Marika sped off at an obedient trot she decided instead to stay outdoors a little longer. The slight breeze was deliciously welcome and her brain was engaged on such frantic activity that she knew she had no hope of sleeping.

Some woman Carlo had loved had betrayed him. Jessica ached at the image of Carlo loving a woman that deeply. It hurt, yes, she acknowledged grudgingly, it really hurt.

Why did that knowledge hurt her? Ego? He had not loved Jessica, had laid no heart at her feet, had made no concessions to her self-respect or pride and had em-

ployed no heated persuasions. He had offered her the
vacant space in his bed and the time limit of his boredom.
A cool, arrogant, take-it-or-leave-it choice. Was that why
it had been so easy to run away?

Leaning on the terrace railing, she let her cool hands
press against her hot cheeks. She had gone to the
Deangate that day in a colossal rage. Calling into her
father's office, she had found him sitting with his head
in his hands.

'I've sold Amory's,' he had muttered as if he couldn't
quite believe it himself. 'I've sold to Carlo. Without
finance, the firm was going to sink. I had no choice.
Better money in the bank than bankruptcy...and I
suppose your mother will be pleased.'

Like a madwoman, Jessica had hammered on the door
of Carlo's suite. He had opened it himself.

'Take a long, slow deep breath,' Carlo had suggested,
reading her furiously flushed face with ease. 'I gather
your father's told you——'

'How dare you steal Amory's from him?' she had
blitzed.

Carlo had poured her a brandy and handed it to her
in silence.

She had downed it in one, outraged by his cool.

'I didn't steal it, I bought it. For far more than it's
worth in its current state of efficiency,' he had drawled.
'And I am not a man known for my generosity. If it
weren't for you, I wouldn't have bought. Your father
doesn't realise how fortunate he is to possess such an
asset.'

'What the hell have I got to do with it?'

'If you had surrendered *last* week,' Carlo had spelt
out gently, 'I would have given him the finance he
requires to survive and he would still have owned
his business.'

Sick with horror, Jessica had stared back at him. He had cruelly laid the responsibility for the loss of Amory's on her shoulders. And there had been worse to come.

'This week, as you may have guessed, that offer was concluded and I bought instead,' he had continued lazily. 'And by next week, I will no longer be prepared to consider offering your father the opportunity of staying on as managing director——'

'That's blackmail,' she had whispered incredulously.

'That's business,' Carlo had asserted.

And Jessica had gone crazy, appalled and outraged that he could use her father to pressure her. A violent row had ensued. She had been so furious, she had no memory of her abuse, but Carlo had lost his temper too. Her attempt to slap his face had landed her on her back on the sofa with Carlo on top of her...and then it had begun, in raw mutual anger that, terrifyingly swiftly, had turned into the scorching heat of an uncontrollable passion.

A passion that was insanity to her in the aftermath of shame and disbelief. But he had not held her down and forced her to submit to his mouth and the heated caress of his hands. She had been a full participant. Hating him, wanting him, needing him, hating herself. He had unleashed a woman she did not know and did not want to remember afterwards. When they were interrupted, she had been fathoms deep in shock.

But Carlo had blazed with triumph. He had skated an insolently intimate hand across her breast in an arrogant display of sexual possession. 'You tell Turner tonight. It's over now. Why did you fight me? From the first, I *knew* it would come to this.'

And she had lain there listening while she died inside at both what she had almost done and what he wanted to make of her. She had hated Carlo with boiling ferocity at that moment of biting humiliation. She had been repulsed by the future he had offered her so casually.

But that had not been why she had run out of the Deangate like a madwoman.

No, far from it. She had run in terror from her own physical response to Carlo, absolutely convinced that she was as oversexed and immoral as her mother. Carlo had been the very first temptation she had ever had to withstand and she had not withstood him. From the moment he touched her she had been a lost cause, burning with a passion that equalled his and utterly, hopelessly submerged in her own sexuality. And then, she acknowledged, she had not been able to cope with that discovery.

Only maturity had brought her closer to understanding. She was a normal healthy woman but for six years she had been forced to repress and deny all her physical urges. Simon's complete indifference to her as a woman had been deeply wounding on every level, a secret shame that had destroyed her faith in her own femininity. Carlo had taught her that she had sexual needs but she had been bitterly ashamed and afraid of those same needs at the age of twenty.

But she owed no other man loyalty now, and why should she be ashamed, she suddenly asked herself angrily—why should she be ashamed of experiencing the natural physical promptings of that side of her nature? Sexual attraction made the world go round. Without it, the human race would die out.

She was not like her mother, ready to jump into bed with any man who took her fancy, she told herself fiercely. If she had been like Carole she would have found it out by now, would have experienced this attraction with a whole host of other men and would surely have ended up having affairs. That she had not told her that she was not as vulnerable as she had once feared, no... not vulnerable at all in that sense.

Take Carlo out of the picture and she could live like a nun. Only Carlo could turn her inside out with one burning glance, only Carlo had the ability to infiltrate her mind with erotic thoughts and melt her to molten honey in his arms. For the very first time in her life she was attempting to understand the sheer driving force of sexual desire and accept it, rather than run in terror and shame from it. But accepting that those promptings existed did not mean that she wanted to act on them.

Slowly, she straightened and made her way back to her bedroom. As she opened the door, she saw that a light was burning. Carlo, minus his jacket and tie, was reclining on her bed.

On the brink of verbal attack she belatedly recalled that she had told him that she wanted to speak to him. 'I gather this is as private as we can get,' she said coolly. 'I had a visit from your stepmother before dinner and very interesting it was too.'

The dark planes of his features were impassive.

'*She* suggested that our engagement was a masquerade and asked me how much you were paying me,' Jessica volunteered. 'She then offered to double it.'

'She was fishing,' Carlo dismissed carelessly.

'Was she? She seemed to be basing her convictions on the belief that we only met for the first time last week——'

'I wonder where she got that from.' But Carlo did not seem particularly interested in the subject, his veiled dark eyes intent on Jessica as she stood there at the foot of the bed. Her heartbeat skidded at the thickening of the atmosphere.

'I told her I'd known you for six years and I think she then assumed that I was suggesting we had been having an affair while I was married but she still thought it was a fairy-story,' Jessica relayed in an increasing rush as Carlo sprang gracefully off the bed and moved towards her. 'What I would like to know is why she was so convinced that we——'

'Ignore her.'

'Carlo, I really would like to go to bed,' she began.

'Your luggage has already been moved.'

Her eyes widened. 'Moved where?'

'My room...where else?' Carlo responded drily, casting open the door in expectation. 'Do you really think it would be credible that we sleep apart?'

But when she had trekked quite to the far side of the villa it occurred to her that *someone* had been very keen to keep them apart, by night at least. Marika?

Carlo had an entire suite of rooms, complete with twin bathrooms. Like an automaton, Jessica took her night attire into one, changed and ten minutes later slid into the wide, empty bed and over to the furthest edge of it. She doubted that some eleventh-hour miracle would save her tonight. Carlo reappeared and shed his towelling robe in an untidy heap on the floor. He looked at her, blazing all-male satisfaction, and she shrank under the sheet.

He stood half in shadow, half in light, the long, muscular planes of his golden body a glorious vision of rampant masculinity, and she felt her own hunger stirring, insidious as a secret invader. Her skin flushed hotly and she closed her eyes, stricken by that hunger and her own sudden blinding shyness.

As he came down on the bed beside her, her mouth ran dry. She felt boneless, scared. Dear God, how was she going to get out of this? If he made love to her, would he be able to tell she was a virgin? Surely not, she told herself, preferring to think of the aftermath rather than what might come before. She had read that a woman's first experience of sex was often a very big disappointment.

Carlo stared down at her in total silence, smouldering golden eyes hungrily scanning her face. Slowly, he raised a blunt forefinger and skimmed it along the voluptuous line of her lower lip. 'Why are you so shy?' he whispered in wonderment.

'S-shy?' She forced a jerky laugh. She could have told him. Every other time he had touched her, he had taken her by surprise. There hadn't been time for considered thought. *This* was different. 'Don't be ridiculous!'

'You look as if you're running a fever, too.' Leaning over her, Carlo flicked one pink cheek mockingly.

'I don't want to do this,' Jessica said fiercely.

'You're no virgin...' Carlo breathed with sudden shocking insolence, his starkly handsome features darkening, brilliant eyes hard. 'You gave that to *him*. You gave to him what should have been mine——'

He was so damn primitive and arrogant. What should have been *his*... how dared he say that after the way he had treated her that day? Did her supposed lack of virginity take the edge off his triumph, dull the pleasure of his conquest? Well, he would never hear from her lips that he had been her first lover. She would take that secret to the grave with her.

'Tough!' The retaliation just erupted from between her clenched teeth.

Dark blood slashed his cheekbones and she paled, knowing instinctively that she had never pushed Carlo closer to violence and realising rather too late that that was the very last mood she wanted him in.

A pair of hard hands sank to her slim hips. He jerked her into the hard heat of his very masculine length, bringing her into direct contact with the full force of his arousal.

'If you hurt me I'll... I'll scream the place down!' Jessica gasped, energised by both that contact and his mood.

'Hurt you? What sort of an animal do you think I am?' Frowning in disbelief, Carlo studied her with probing golden eyes and his sensual mouth firmed.

A very male animal, she thought fearfully.

'I have no intention of hurting you,' Carlo asserted drily, and lowered his dark head.

He took her parted lips in a hot, hungry surge of passion. He knotted a hand into her hair, holding her there as though he feared she might seek to evade him, but the instant their mouths met Jessica went limp, bowing to the inevitable. Within seconds the fear was burned away by the heat of his mouth. She quivered in response, and thought became far too much of a challenge.

He bent his dark head over the full swell of her breasts and her fingers speared helplessly into his thick black hair. His lips pulled on a taut pink nipple and a whimper of sound escaped from her convulsed throat. He lingered there, toying with her sensitive flesh until every skin cell went on red alert and every nerve-ending tautened in sizzling anticipation. Her hands gripped his smooth brown shoulders and skimmed in near-desperation over the tautness of the muscles flexing in his back.

She felt as if she was being consumed. There was no breathing space between one spasm of response and the next. Sensation took over and she was mindless in the grip of it. His mouth on her breast was an unbelievable pleasure, but when he began to employ his tongue and the teasing edge of his teeth she went crazy, possessed by a hunger so intense she was lost to all else. She twisted restively beneath him, too hot to stay still, sobbed out his name, drove her fingers into his hair, wantonly, wildly out of control.

'We have all night,' Carlo muttered thickly, lifting his head.

She focused on him with the blankness of passion's grip and simply, instinctively reached for him again because he had dared to stop and she couldn't bear that.

With a husky laugh, Carlo caught her to him. 'Slow down,' he urged softly.

She ran exploring fingers through the curling black hair on his chest, tracing the superb musculature rippling below his golden skin. She heard the startled hiss of his breath escaping and then he took her hand and thrust it down to the hard swell of his erection, shocking her, startling her.

'Touch me,' he invited with an earthy groan.

He was velvet-smooth and hot and hard and she was helplessly alarmed by the sheer size of him. She looked up at him, dredged from the hold of passion by the bite of her own ignorance and sudden shyness.

Carlo dealt her a sudden vibrantly amused smile and moved against her, pure sexual licence barely contained. 'I'll teach you some time... but what an extraordinary gap in your education.' He punctuated the comment by driving her flat again with the force of his mouth.

Sanity trickled away again like sand through a mesh grid. He kissed her breathless, long, deep, drugging kisses that stole the soul from her body and melted her into a quivering length of subservience.

Only then did he lift his head again and slide with aching slowness down the length of her extended body, making love to every part of her he could reach. The tip of his tongue dipped into her navel and she whimpered with an intolerable desire, jack-knifing wildly under the taunting, teasing fingers skimming her unbearably tender nipples. She couldn't stay still but he forced her still with powerful hands, forcing her to endure every maddening second of his tormenting assault.

Her entire body was possessed by an electrifying excitement and yet simultaneously one gigantic ache expressing the raw agony of her need. By the time he parted her thighs and let knowing fingers brush against the honeyed centre of that ache, she was at screaming pitch and she cried out his name, her hips moving with a rhythm that required no enforced learning. It came as naturally as the air in her lungs.

He was touching her now as she had never been touched and she was on fire, convinced she was being tortured to death by pleasure. She sobbed just to breathe, her heartbeat thundering madly against her breastbone, the blood in her veins racing insanely in accompaniment. She couldn't bear it...

'You're very tight,' Carlo muttered thickly, hesitating.

Her body was at screaming pitch. Instinctively she pulled him down to her, desperate for contact, any form of continuing contact. Untensing, he followed her lead, his hands tipping her up, spreading her thighs. He entered her with one fierce thrust and then stilled, every muscle ferociously taut as he groaned with the nakedness of his pleasure. It hurt so much, Jessica almost passed out with the sheer shock of being forced back to reality.

She twisted her head away to hide her reaction, thankfully feeling the edge of the pain fade away. Carlo uttered a feverish imprecation and stopped.

'I'm hurting you——'

'*No!*'

'Relax then,' he instructed unevenly.

Pushing his hands beneath her hips, he plunged deeper still into her damp sheath in a rawly powerful invasion. This time there was no pain. In fact he dragged a sob of incredulous delight from her. The pleasure came back in powerful waves, shooting through her in a rejuvenating burst of energy.

He moved with restraint and then slowly, he began to drive into her harder and faster with a shuddering savagery that sent her finally rocketing into an explosive climax of such intensity that a wild cry escaped her and her quivering body writhed uncontrollably under the hard onslaught of his. Groaning her name, Carlo slammed into her one last time and then jerked violently with the force of his own release.

Rolling on to his back, Carlo carried her with him, binding her into his arms so tightly she could barely breathe. Jessica was in a daze, a complete daze, and she lay like a boneless rag doll on top of him, her face buried in the hollow of one broad shoulder, her nostrils flaring sensuously at the hot, moist scent of him.

She was in seventh heaven. In the back of her mind she was already wondering when he would do it again. Her face burned. She was a shameless hussy but she couldn't help it. Nothing could have prepared her for that amount of pleasure. Still in shock at her own response, she felt drugged and incapable, incredibly tender towards him.

Her mouth curved in a silent caress against his bronzed skin. And then it hit her like a bolt of lightning. I love him. A quiver of disbelief ran through her. Carlo instantly tautened his grip on her. I love every rotten thing about him, she registered in growing horror. His temper, his arrogance, his sheer bloody persistence. Mentally, she felt like the ground had suddenly vanished from beneath her feet. The silence began to get to her in her new and tender state of vulnerability.

Carlo was thinking. Strange, how she could literally *feel* Carlo thinking manipulative thoughts, practically see all those little cogs and wheels spinning ever faster in that far too clever brain of his.

'Extraordinary,' Carlo murmured softly. 'You felt like a virgin. If it were not for that ring you used to wear, I would be one hundred per cent convinced I had just become your first lover.'

Tense as a bow string, Jessica uttered a strangled laugh. 'Don't be ridiculous——'

'Was I hallucinating? I hurt you——'

She tensed in horror. 'You were rough,' she muttered hurriedly.

Carlo shifted lithely on to his side, taking her with him. She collided with the full force of blazing golden eyes and paled but she was still determined to silence the smallest suspicion he might have. 'It's been a very long time since——'

'Rough...' Carlo sent her a slashing, primal look of thwarted fury and abruptly freed her. He sprang out of bed. 'I need a shower.'

She turned over and found a cool spot on the pillow. Not the most generous of comments, she registered belatedly, scarlet washing her cheekbones. Oh, what a tangled web, she thought guiltily. Deception didn't come naturally to her but a current of fierce pride and loyalty to Simon's memory kept her silent.

'What the hell is this?'

The wrathful incredulity in Carlo's growled demand lifted her pale head. At arms length, Carlo extended a framed photo. He was possessed by such ferocious incredulity, he couldn't hold it steady.

It was of Simon. Her jaw dropped. It had been at the foot of her overnight bag, one of the pieces of luggage she had packed to come here. She had not intended to bring it, indeed had completely forgotten its existence until this moment.

'Where did you get it?' she demanded.

'It was on the dressing-table!' Carlo unleashed, spitting out every syllable with a flash of white teeth.

'I didn't put it there!'

'But you brought it out here with you!' Carlo seethed, flinging it violently aside. 'Into my bedroom——'

'I did not bring it into your bedroom!' Jessica gasped unsteadily.

Carlo strode forward and swooped on her in a tempest of rage. He scared her half to death and she fought with flailing arms and flying fists to fight him off. He dropped her from a height on to a sofa that had all the bounce of a rock. 'You sleep here...I do not want you in my bed!' he delivered.

She was stark naked and absolutely humiliated. He yanked a blanket out of a closet and threw it at her. Clumsily hauling it round her, she headed for the door. 'I am not staying here to be insulted...you primitive bloody man!' she scorched back at him.

'You put one toe in that corridor and the electronic surveillance picks you up on camera. My father's security men will have one hell of a laugh. Go ahead!'

She hesitated and then snatched her fingers back from the door-handle as though she had been burnt. Without a single glance in his direction, she made it back to the sofa, rigid-backed but literally shaking with the force of her own fury.

'I thought you might see it that way,' Carlo drawled with blatant amusement, temper cooled by the ridiculous picture she made. 'Learn to look on sleeping in my bed in my arms as a privilege——'

'You hateful bastard!' Jessica screamed back at him.

'And by the way…you love it rough!' Carlo shot at her for good measure.

'*Shut up, Carlo!*'

I do not love him, she told herself ferociously, huddling into a ball, the blanket tangled uncomfortably round her. I do not love him. I hate him! I hate him so much I could burst wide open with it! *He's jealous.* Carlo was wildly jealous of Simon. How come it had taken her this long to appreciate something that obvious? In the darkness, she smiled, fists unclenching. She didn't care if she didn't sleep a wink. She was fairly certain that he wouldn't either.

CHAPTER SEVEN

LUNCH was being served outdoors beneath the leafy splendour of a ring of flame trees. Beyond them, flight after flight of shallow steps adorned with classical statues descended to the white beach below. Lukas Philippides dealt Jessica a fiercely amused scrutiny. Flustered, she dropped down into her seat. One of the maids had awakened her and she hadn't had much time to get ready.

When she glanced up again, Carlo's brilliant golden eyes were wandering with indolent satisfaction over her in a look as blatantly physical as a caress. A deep flush of awareness carmined her skin, making her desperately conscious of the unfamiliar ache between her thighs. Erotic recollections surfaced and she fought them to the last ditch, feverishly embarrassed by her own lack of mental discipline.

While she slept, Carlo had shifted her off the sofa and back into his bed. Out of consideration for her comfort and his own unjustifiable behaviour the night before...or out of a need to set the scene to keep their deception intact? At what stage had she chosen to overlook the fact that it had always been Carlo's stated intent to make love to her for the benefit of that self-same deception? A deep unease assailed Jessica. Now they *were* lovers, she was far more powerfully aware of the masquerade they were engaged in and she was forced to question Carlo's motives.

Was Carlo simply trying to please his dying father? Or was there a far more mercenary reasoning behind it all? Yesterday she had tried very hard not to think about that. Today, she found that she could think of little else.

Sunny sauntered up, clad in a flowing dress and sunhat, looking vaguely reminiscent of a Twenties film starlet on a picnic. Picturesque and quite stunningly beautiful, she took her seat. Both Lukas and Carlo had watched her progress across the lawn. You had to hand it to her, Jessica thought sourly. Sunny knew how to make an entrance.

Last night, Jessica had wondered if Sunny had a problem with drink and if that might explain her strange visit to her room and her even stranger remarks. But she hadn't behaved then as though she had been over-indulging. Neither her speech nor her movement had been impaired. Yet Carlo had been surprisingly uncon-cerned by his stepmother's conviction that their en-gagement was a fake.

'A toast…' Lukas announced, raising his glass of wine. 'To Carlo and Jessica. The wedding will take place on Tuesday.'

Jessica's hand jerked and sent her glass over. A pool of red wine spread across the white tablecloth. She col-lided with Carlo's hooded dark eyes and read the warning there. To say nothing, do nothing.

Sunny sighed and laid a soft hand on her husband's sleeve. 'I think you've shocked your son, Lukas. Don't you think this should be *his* decision?' she prompted with a small, deprecating smile. 'I hope you don't mind me speaking up——'

Lukas shook off her hand irritably. 'Since when have I wanted your opinion on anything?' he demanded rudely.

'My thanks,' Carlo murmured softly into the throbbing silence. 'But Jessica and I are not intending to marry until next year.'

'This year, next year!' Lukas responded with abrasive bite. 'You think to deprive me of a father's right to see his son marry?' It was a thunderous demand of disbelief.

Carlo tautened, his dark features clenching hard. He said something in Greek but Lukas slashed a despotic hand through the air and retorted in English, hot temper flushing his drawn face at the threat of his authority being further challenged.

'Enough!' he ground out angrily. 'It is arranged. Already the invitations go out. You people! A little surprise and where is your gratitude?'

As his bloodshot gaze raked the table, seeking dissension, Jessica studied the stained tablecloth. Dear heaven, why hadn't either she or Carlo seen the threat of this in advance? Lukas Philippides was dying. It was surely not that unreasonable of him to want the wedding of his son to take place here and now while he could still enjoy it? So simple, so understandable a wish, that she marvelled that such a danger had not previously occurred to either of them. But somehow, heaven knew how, she conceded dazedly, Carlo was going to have to get them back out of this tight corner! And he only had three days in which to accomplish that feat . . .

'We will fly to Miami to find a dress,' Marika announced cheerfully.

'You pick a designer,' Lukas interrupted with a curled lip. 'But he will fly here.'

'I really cannot arrange a wedding in that timespan,' Sunny said thinly, coldly.

'What's it got to do with you?' Lukas snorted. 'Marika will take care of it all.'

It was without doubt the most strained meal Jessica had ever endured. When Lukas went off to rest, as was apparently his habit in the afternoon, she left the table with relief and started for the steps.

'Jessica . . .'

Halfway down, she spun, stilled by Carlo's voice. He drew level with her, very tall and very lean and very dark and quite extravagantly gorgeous in the first casual clothing she had ever seen him in. Faded jeans sleekly encased his narrow hips and long, powerful legs, a short-sleeved cotton shirt open at his brown throat. Hurriedly, Jessica dragged her gaze from him. And then, above at the top of the steps, she saw Sunny standing there, watching them. She looked furious.

'And how do you plan to get us out of the wedding?' Jessica enquired tightly.

Carlo threw back his black head and suddenly laughed. 'I don't!'

She couldn't believe what she was hearing and looked back at him in shock.

'The only escape would be to tell the truth,' Carlo pointed out gently. 'And that is quite out of the question.'

'You could tell him that you're not sure of your feelings for me!' Jessica protested tautly.

Carlo moved on down the steps in front of her. 'That would be the very last excuse I would offer——'

'*But why*?' Jessica demanded in furious frustration. 'He's been married four times himself! Surely he would understand?'

Carlo didn't respond. Infuriatingly, he moved fluidly on down to the beach. She caught up with him breathlessly.

'Let's go sailing,' he suggested lazily as if the previous conversation had been most definitely concluded.

'*Carlo*!' Jessica gritted, struggling to match her pace to the long stride heading in the direction of the wooden jetty where a large and immaculate white yacht was moored.

'We get married, then we divorce,' Carlo breathed impatiently. 'No big deal!'

Jessica couldn't credit his attitude. 'It's a heck of a big deal to me!'

Carlo stilled and scanned her with hooded dark eyes. 'Really, *cara*? You married Turner without love... why not me?'

Attacked by such open derision, she paled.
'That...that isn't true.'

'If you had really loved him, you would never have
allowed me to lay a finger upon you,' Carlo murmured
drily.

'You're trying to change the subject——'

'Why should I need to? We made a deal. Three months
of your freedom,' Carlo reminded her, his sunbronzed
profile hardening. 'And having seen my father, I think
it highly unlikely that he will survive half that period.'

Involuntarily, she felt his pain at that estimation. It
was there in his roughened voice and tautening features,
but Jessica felt that pain on a deeper level, her own
feelings for Carlo heightening her sensitivity. He really
did care about his father. For the first time, she acknowledged that truth and the unlikelihood of Carlo's
cherishing purely mercenary motives for their fake engagement. Maybe it was all just as it seemed on the
surface. Lukas was delighted at the idea of Carlo marrying and Carlo was prepared to pretend to give that
pleasure.

'I'm sorry,' she muttered, her throat thickening. 'You
must wish you had come here years ago——'

'No. It is only working now on these terms,' Carlo
retorted flatly. 'Lukas and I have never got on. I believe
it is often so with father and son. Only the lack of time
brings us together. It makes me more tolerant and him
more generous...'

With a mighty effort of will, she fought an over-
whelming urge to close her arms round him. 'You must
have known that he might demand that you marry
me——'

'Yes.' Carlo shrugged a shoulder with Latin casu-
alness. 'It is a small thing if it contents him.'

'But it is not a small thing to me, Carlo.' They were
strolling towards the yacht.

She stared down at the sea, deep blue and then blindingly silver where the sun's glare hit the water. One false marriage was enough in any woman's life. She refused to make a second. What Carlo wished to do to placate his father was his business, she told herself, staving off an unwilling stab of sympathy. He had no right to ask such a thing from her, especially when he coolly admitted that he had foreseen this situation arising and had not bothered to warn her.

'I will not hold you a day after his death.'

The assurance hit her like a cruel blow and she despised herself for reeling from that reality as though it were a surprise. She loved him, hopelessly, helplessly, but that did not mean making a sacrificial lamb of herself. Some day not too far in the future, Lukas would die and it would all be over. The deception would end, and with it the affair. She did not want a fake wedding-ring to add to her bitterness.

But didn't she owe Carlo something for the immense kindness and tact he had employed with her *own* father? OK, they had made a deal but Carlo could have fulfilled the terms far less generously. A deal... dear God, she reflected painfully, had the giving of her body last night merely been part of the deal as well? Her stomach heaved at the suspicion.

Carlo planted his hands to her waist, taking her by surprise, and swung her with ease on to the gleaming wooden deck of the yacht. Two crewmen emerged. The men talked and Jessica planted her unsteady hands on the shining brass guard rail. Drawn by a need she could not suppress, her troubled gaze clung to Carlo's strong, masculine profile. He was such a mixture of opposites. Kind and cruel. Understanding and judgemental. Tender and rough. Quick-tempered, calculating, secretive but capable of far more true emotions than she had ever believed. And he hated her.

He hated her for marrying another man. She had cast a slur on his manhood, injured his precious pride and he was still seething with a sense of injustice. But how many women would have thrown themselves gratefully into his arms six years ago after the treatment she had received? And by what God given right did Carlo imagine that she should have swallowed such arrogance when on every other level they had been mortal enemies? Yet she could not imagine Carlo behaving now as he had behaved then.

'Do you like sailing?' Linking his arms round her, Carlo drew her back into disturbing connection with every vibrant line of his long, muscular length.

'I haven't done much.' Feeling manipulated, Jessica stiffened, fighting the flood of heat threatening to consume her. 'Don't change the subject.'

'There is nothing more to say,' he breathed, pressing her closer still, the palm of one lean hand splaying across her taut stomach as he bent over her. 'There is also little that I would not do to assuage my father's fear——'

'Fear?' She frowned.

Perceptibly, he tensed. 'His fear that I might not marry——'

'But why should he fear that?' She wanted him to tell her what his sister had already told her.

'As a man who married for the first time as a teenager, he cannot comprehend my single state.'

Disappointment assailed her. He was lying to her…or at the very least mounting a cover-up. He did not confide in her. It shook her that they could have shared something so intimate last night and yet he could still hold her at a distance. Her own emotions were not similarly disciplined. She had lost all ability to stand back and be rational. She was too involved now.

'He doesn't seem particularly happy in his own marriage,' she said drily.

'Sunny is forty years his junior. Would you expect a match made in heaven? He's content enough. He only ever looked for two things from your sex. An ability to decorate the bedroom, and to reproduce.'

Jessica was chilled. Presumably Sunny had married for money and position but she reckoned that the redhead paid for her pleasures. Now she asked herself if Carlo wanted any more from a woman than his father ever had. Right now, Carlo was using her, and last night he had used her body as well. Why didn't she face that harsh reality head-on?

He had brought her here to pretend to be his fiancée but she was being forced into deeper deception with every hour that passed. And he had yet to explain *why* to her satisfaction. How did she know whether or not his principal motivation was connected with the terms of his inheritance? He wasn't going to admit it, was he?

And suddenly, she wondered if that might be why Sunny had attempted to the best of her limited influence over Lukas to hold off the wedding ... why Sunny might have been so keen to prove that their engagement was a fake. Were Carlo and Sunny competing in the same competition? How was Lukas's immense wealth tied up?

The blood chilled in Jessica's veins. She didn't know what to think, swerved from one moment to the next, but now she recognised how much making love with Carlo had increased her sense of insecurity. She could live with the deception if it was just a matter of pleasing a dying man ... she could not live with it or herself on any other terms. It would be too unbearably, cruelly humiliating.

'You're astoundingly quiet.' Without warning, his lean brown hands moved up to her breasts, cupping them, and she quivered violently, her rigidity evaporating in a surge of heat.

'You're wearing a bra,' he complained.

'Don't!' she gasped, sudden tears lashing the back of her eyes. Dear lord, she felt so vulnerable now. She craved his touch helplessly but then she wondered how much *this* meant to him. A little light relief on an island where there was no other sexual outlet for his desires, or did he get even more of a kick out of her wanton response? Revenge...how much did that play a part in his apparent hunger for her?

Dropping his hands, Carlo spun her easily round to face him. Surprising lines of strain were engraved between his expressive mouth and arrogant nose. She met dark golden eyes that riveted her bonelessly in place. 'I want to forget Paradiso and its occupants for an afternoon.' Carlo pushed back the silver hair curving her cheekbones and framed her uncertain face with both hands. 'When I make love with you, I forget everything else. It is the sweetest oblivion I know,' he stated huskily.

Her heart jumped behind her breastbone. She turned to watch the two crewmen unfurling the sails, wretchedly aware of just how badly she wanted to believe him. The yacht sailed round Paradiso. Since the cay encompassed little more than a square mile of territory that didn't take long. Jessica let Carlo show her down into a comfortable cabin and display the range of swimwear available for her use. She took her time selecting a bikini in the least daring design. When she climbed the companionway, she saw the crewmen speeding away in the motorboat.

'Why have they gone?'

'To leave us in privacy,' Carlo advanced, amused by her question, intent golden eyes lazily skimming over the full thrust of her breasts and the rounded swell of her hips.

A deep flush warmed her skin.

He stripped off his shirt and cast it carelessly aside.

He had a truly magnificent torso. Her tongue stole out to moisten her dry lips as he embarked on his jeans.

She expected him to reveal swimming briefs beneath but Carlo skimmed off down to bare golden flesh. 'I never wear anything when I'm swimming.'

'So I see.' Magnetised by the view, she stared like a schoolgirl as he executed a perfect dive off the yacht and broke into a fast crawl that cut through the water.

A less able swimmer, she got into the water by way of the steps provided. The sea was deliciously warm. After a little exercise, she let herself float, heat beating down on her wet body like a rejuvenating drug.

Carlo surfaced beside her. 'You're not very active.'

'Don't pull me under or anything smart like that!' she warned nervously.

He kissed her instead, and in the sudden blinding grip of sensation she forgot to paddle and was hauled upright again by Carlo before she slid beneath the surface. 'Float,' he suggested gently, amusedly.

Half an hour later, she was reclining on a sun-lounger, a Daiquiri clasped in one hand, as she let relaxation seep luxuriously through her every limb. She opened her eyes behind her sunglasses when the glorious heat was abruptly reduced by Carlo's arrangement of a parasol above her. 'Spoilsport,' she muttered.

'You'll burn...and if you burn,' Carlo said with single-minded cool, 'I won't be able to touch you.'

'I would prefer to burn——'

'Liar.' He reached for her with hands that brooked no argument and she trembled as the sunwarmed heat of his body met electrifyingly with hers. He had dispensed with the towel he had knotted round his lean hips.

'Don't you think you should put some clothes on?' she gasped.

'I think you need a few anatomy lessons,' he laughed softly, indolently, scanning her hot cheeks. 'Did he undress in the dark?'

'That is a disgusting question!' Jessica was suddenly infuriated by the sheer blaze of his sexual confidence.

Did he think desire would make a mindless slave out of her? Did he think he could use sex to blind her to everything else?

'And to return to the subject you keep dropping,' she snapped. 'I don't want to go through with a fake wedding.'

Carlo gazed down at her and slowly, erotically moved on her, forcing her into raw acquaintance with his arousal. 'Sometimes we all have to do things we don't want to do.'

'Meaning that you don't either?' In quite irrational annoyance, her mouth tightened as she fought to suppress the shivering hunger he was invoking in her with such insulting ease.

'A wedding-ring has to be about the last reward I would want to give you——'

Her amethyst eyes widened to their fullest extent. '*Reward*? You consider going through a disgusting parody of a wedding ceremony a reward?'

Untouched by her fury, Carlo cast her a grim smile. 'Parody or not, it will still be a true marriage and you will still be my wife...for a while.'

'You smirking, self-satisfied toad!' Jessica launched up at him. 'You think that's a reward? It's a punishment! Unlike you, I have some respect for the sacrament of marriage. It's not just a useful ploy to me...you'd use anything and anybody to get what you want!'

Hooded dark eyes surveyed her. Abruptly, he lifted himself fluidly from her and vaulted upright, contempt in every angle of his bearing. 'Would I?' he parried drily. 'Six years ago, I could have told your father how *close* we had become and I am quite sure he would have strained every sinew sooner than watch you marry Turner!'

Her furious gaze dropped from him. She had never thought of that possibility. His derisive withdrawal exercised a similarly disturbing effect on her. She felt bereft.

'I could have personally dealt with Turner. I could have made marrying you such a humiliation that *he* would have been forced to save face by calling off the wedding!' Carlo continued with biting conviction. 'I did neither of those things. I kept quiet. I stood back...I allowed you to make your own decision——'

'Damn you!' Jessica gasped. 'There was no decision. You treated me like a whore!'

'That is not true.'

'Yes, it is. And don't you dare forget the background of blackmail and pressure that came before it!' Jessica urged bitterly. 'I never have. You made no attempt to understand how I felt. I had betrayed Simon. I had done something unforgivable to a man I believed I loved. I was confused and ashamed and I couldn't handle it. And what did you do? You gloated. You didn't care about how anybody felt, except yourself. You said that was true of your father but it was equally true of you then!'

Carlo was standing stock-still, his piercing gaze wholly pinned to her distressed face. 'You said...the man you *believed* you loved. So you finally admit it,' he grated, throwing his ebony head back. 'You finally admit that you didn't love him.'

Jessica whirled away, cursing her impulsive tongue and the descent into temper which removed all restraint. Her knuckles showed white as she curved her unsteady hands fiercely round the rail. 'I thought I loved him...later I realised that I didn't...at least,' she stumbled in her turmoil, 'not the way I should have loved him.'

'Later!' Carlo ejaculated with lancing contempt. He followed it up with something that sounded exceedingly rude in Greek.

In anguish, Jessica closed her eyes, breathing deeply. She had loved Simon as a friend. Had their marriage been normal, she might have continued to believe that she loved him, but when they had lived month after month with separate bedrooms and the relationship of a brother and sister, she had had too much time in which to analyse the fact that sexually Simon did not attract her and that, if she offered herself, tried to talk to him about the lack of a physical relationship, she did it out of guilt and the belief that that willingness was the very least she owed him. Ironically, that attitude had kept Simon at even more of a distance until he fell ill and sex became the least of their worries, she conceded sadly.

'I did not treat you like a whore——'

'Ten days ago, you called me one for what we did that day! And that is how you treated me,' she condemned starkly, sticking to her point. 'I was only twenty and I had no experience of a man like you. You are the one who took advantage, Carlo——'

'I wanted you.' The assurance was harsh, immoveable, no admission of fault.

Her mouth twisted painfully. 'Regardless of cost or decency? I paid in spades for what I did. Loyalty is very important to me. I could hardly live with myself and all for what...a little entertainment for you, so that you could prove that I *was* susceptible? Was it worth it?' she demanded shakily.

'No,' he murmured, suddenly very quiet. 'Looking back, I see that it was not worth the cost.'

Involuntarily she looked at him. His chiselled profile might have been carved from marble. All of a sudden she wanted him to argue the point, which was crazy. He should never have touched her that day but then neither one of them had been in control. She saw that now. Carlo had been as possessed as she was by the passion that had flared up between them. But that didn't mean she forgave him for his behaviour afterwards.

He sailed the yacht back in alone. She couldn't wait to get off it. She couldn't cope with Carlo's moody introspection. Silence from Carlo was not golden. She felt shut out, banished. She had the lowering suspicion that he could barely bring himself to look at her and without the false strength of anger and bitterness over the past she found that she was weak and horribly vulnerable to the chill in the air.

She spent ages getting ready for dinner, lazing in a bath for a full hour and fussing unnecessarily with her hair. The dress she chose was black. It suited her mood, a long dark sheath hugging every curve. She would rival Sunny, she thought wryly.

Lukas was absent from the dinner-table. 'He's resting in bed,' Marika explained. 'There has been too much excitement.'

Sunny, brilliant as a butterfly in emerald lace, laughed thinly. 'Excitement? Here on this godforsaken rock? You've got to be joking!'

'This is a difficult time for all of us,' Marika murmured.

'He's dying but I might as well be dead too,' Sunny complained bitterly. 'I hate this place.'

'Nobody's keeping you here.' Marika's plump face was flushed with rare anger.

'Well, thank you very much!' Shooting Marika a look of outrage, Sunny rose from the table and stalked from the room.

'I should not have said that,' Marika whispered in distress, tears blurring her brown eyes.

Carlo said something in Greek and patted his sister's hand. She squeezed his fingers gratefully, her lips wobbling into a rueful smile.

'I shall go and sit with Lukas,' Carlo announced before dessert was served. He strode out of the room without a backward glance in Jessica's direction.

Jessica went off to explore after dinner, wandering through beautifully furnished and decorated reception rooms that were lifeless. She was delighted to come upon a library and, locating the English section, selected a Jane Austen she hadn't read for several years. But Miss Austen failed her for the very first time. Jessica found it impossible to concentrate.

Standing up again, she cast the novel aside and stepped through the curtains to open the french windows that featured in virtually every room. She walked along the terrace. As she passed by open doors, she caught Sunny's voice clear as a bell.

'You can't love her, Carlo... you *can't* possibly love her!' she was arguing shrilly. 'And he can't force you to marry her!'

'Control yourself,' Carlo breathed fiercely. 'Have you any idea what he would do to you if he knew you were here with me?'

'You want me... not her!' Sunny told him. 'I love you... you know I do! Look at the risks I've taken!'

Carlo said something that might have been a swear word.

Jessica had stopped dead in her tracks. There was a curious ringing in her eardrums. She couldn't breathe. The curtains weren't drawn. She could see them. Carlo had his back to her. Sunny had flung herself into a chair to sob hysterically.

'Why don't you tell him that you don't want to marry her?' she demanded wildly. 'You're the only one of us who can afford to stand up to him. He'll give you whatever you want.'

'I doubt very much that that includes his wife, cast-off or otherwise,' Carlo said very drily.

'God forgive me, I can't wait for him to die!' Sunny sobbed.

CHAPTER EIGHT

An involuntary moan escaped Jessica and Carlo spun fluidly round. But by then Jessica had already fled, her sole desire to escape. She raced down the steps that led into the gardens, her breath sobbing in her throat.

'Jessica!'

Lights came on, illuminating the outdoors. Jessica kept on running blindly, heedless of the shrubs that tore at her. The heel of one of her shoes snapped when she stumbled. She kicked it off and then bent to rip off the other one. She headed for the steps that would take her to the beach, down and down and down again, far too fast for safety but truly not caring whether or not she fell and hurt herself. Carlo was behind her. She could hear his pursuit and she moved as if the devil were on her heels.

She tore on to the beach and instantly into the cloaking cover of the trees, struggling desperately not to gasp for oxygen, her hand crammed against her convulsing mouth.

'Jessica!' Carlo roared, and she froze in her hiding place.

She watched him stride down the beach, lean hands on hips, a desperate urgency in his very aggressive movement. Maybe he would tie a big rock to her ankle and drown her if he found her. The secret she had learnt was undoubtedly the biggest danger he had ever faced. He moved off towards the jetty and immediately she set off again in the opposite direction.

Her dress tore on a branch, scraping her abdomen painfully. Pulling free, she kept going until she couldn't keep going any longer. Her breasts heaving with the effort of breathing, she collapsed where she stood. The agony folded in and she shuddered and shook, hugging herself with trembling arms, rocking back and forth without realising it.

Carlo and Sunny. His father's wife. It was obscene, unbearable. How could she have been so blind? Sunny hadn't been confused when she came to Jessica's room. Sunny had known that Jessica was simply a pawn on the board. Did Lukas suspect that his wife and his son were having an affair? Was that why Jessica had been required as a smoke-screen for this visit?

Jessica covered her face and wanted to die. No wonder Sunny had attempted to hold off the wedding. She was in love with Carlo. Dear God...no wonder Carlo had refused to tell her the truth. No decent human being would have agreed to such a deception.

Carlo was even prepared to go to the lengths of marrying her to be convincing! Carlo had made love to her last night while the woman he really loved slept under the same roof. Jessica was a mass of pain and wounded emotion. Sunny had been responsible for that room miles away from Carlo. Sunny had been jealous. Sunny hadn't wanted the deception to go that far. But then Carlo was cleverer. Carlo had been determined to play the masquerade for real for his shrewd father's benefit. And he hadn't drawn the line at driving poor, stupid Jessica mad with desire and ensuring that she fulfilled the agreement to the very last letter.

A twig snapped. That was her only warning. Her swollen eyes opened. Carlo was hunkered down in front of her. 'Go away!' she gasped.

He ignored her. An unexpectedly gentle hand lifted one of her bare feet and he groaned. 'You've cut your feet to ribbons...you're bleeding!'

Dimly she was aware of the stinging of her maltreated flesh but it was her heart and her pride and her ability to trust that was causing her the most unimaginable pain. She bowed her head down on her raised knees, tight as a spring with tension.

Carlo swore succinctly. 'Come here!' A powerful hand closed round one scratched forearm.

'No!' Her voice broke right down the middle as she reeled back, desperate to avoid the contact.

'I have the feeling that I have been condemned to Death Row without the right to appeal.'

'That's w-where you ought to be!' she condemned strickenly. 'It's vile! The two of you waiting like ghouls for him to die ... I feel dirty, dear God, I feel soiled and you w-wouldn't believe how dumb and stupid I feel!'

She loved him. That was the full extent of her stupidity. She deserved everything that had happened to her. She deserved to be used and abused. Her own pride and self-discipline should have protected her.

Carlo expelled his breath in a hiss and leapt upright again. His lean powerful length was rigid.

'Just g-get me off this island!' Jessica sobbed.

'Isn't life a bitch?' Carlo breathed. 'The woman I don't want is obsessed by me and the woman I do want spends her whole time running in the wrong direction.'

It was too late. Didn't he see that? Was his estimation of her intelligence so low that he could think he could fool her again?

'*Dio* ... what sort of bastard do you think I am?' he demanded with sudden ferocious hostility.

'I suppose if it weren't for the money the two of you would have got together openly a long time ago,' Jessica mumbled sickly.

'Would you just listen to me?' he demanded rawly.

He was about to tell the truth and she didn't want to hear it. She did not want to hear how his love for Sunny had overcome family loyalty and every decent feeling. 'I don't want to know!' she burst out. 'Not any of it!'

'I could beat you for that,' Carlo bit out with blatant frustration. 'There is nothing between Sunny and me. There never has been. There never will be.'

That did grab her attention. She lifted her tear-swollen face and stared. Carlo was standing several feet away, the moonlight picking out the grim lines of his darkly handsome features.

'It didn't sound like that.'

'Six months ago, I met Sunny for the first time at a party in Rome. She knew Lukas was dying. She's been chasing me ever since——'

'Chasing you?' Jessica echoed.

'The first couple of times I ran into her, I took her out to dinner, purely and simply because she's my father's wife,' Carlo spelt out with sardonic bite. 'But Sunny read that differently. She took it as encouragement. She showed up at my apartment one night in London and asked for a bed for the night, told me this stupid story about being afraid to stay in a hotel alone since some friend of hers was raped. I fell for it... but the only bed Sunny wanted into was mine...'

Jessica swallowed hard. 'And?'

'She told me she was in love with me and I had her driven to a hotel in the middle of the night. But Sunny's very persistent because no man has ever rejected her,' Carlo murmured with an expressive grimace. 'Sunny is one of the reasons I brought you here. I wanted her kept at a distance——'

'So you needed me as a... a buffer——'

'It would be a little difficult for her to get into my bed when it was already occupied,' Carlo said very drily.

Bemusedly, she struggled to recall what Carlo had said in that emotional scene she had stumbled on, and she realised that Carlo had said nothing that did not fit the story he had told her. Her head ached at the effort of concentration. She was almost afraid to give way to the intensity of her relief.

'She's so beautiful,' she muttered.

Carlo said nothing. In the silence, all she could hear was the thunder of her own heart and the soft rushing of the surf.

'A storm in a teacup, then,' she said uncomfortably. 'I'm sorry, I assumed——'

'The worst? Don't you always?' Carlo drawled.

As he extended a lean hand down to her, Jessica allowed him to pull her up. The force of her distress had left her badly shaken. Relieved as she had been by Carlo's confidences, she still felt frighteningly raw and vulnerable. Badly needing to believe that he did not find Sunny desirable, she looked up into his hard features but she could read nothing there, knew that what Carlo did not volunteer, she would never guess. Carlo did not easily reveal his emotions.

He tugged her back along the beach. She could feel the pain in her abused feet now and the sting of the scratches on her arms and stomach. At the foot of the steps, he surveyed her limping gait and groaned. Bending, he hoisted her over one shoulder.

'You *can't* carry me up there!' she objected.

But he did, although by the time they reached the top every muscle in his superbly built body was feverishly taut and she could feel the dampness of perspiration sticking his silk shirt to his skin. 'No more steps,' he muttered raggedly.

He set her down in the lift that gave his father access to the gardens and sent the doors winging shut. He lounged back fluidly against the stainless steel wall and surveyed her with sudden uninhibited intensity.

The dark vibrancy of his magnetism was potent. Jessica collided with smouldering golden eyes and her heart skipped a beat and began to race instead. A slow, sensual smile curved his handsome mouth. He reached out and deftly flicked open the control panel. He touched a button and the lift swooshed to a halt and he hit another before the doors could open.

Arranged on the wall opposite, Jessica felt a quivering heaviness enter her lower limbs as Carlo closed the distance between them. He braced his hands on either side of her and drove her head back with the force of his mouth, his kiss like a fiery brand of ownership. He unleashed a hunger that was primitive in its intensity, sending a burst of scorching heat shooting through her veins.

'Somebody might——' she gasped as he released her reddened lips.

'If I don't have you now,' Carlo said thickly, 'I'll die.'

His hands wrenched down the straps of her sleeveless dress and she glanced down, shocked to see her own bared breasts, helplessly shy of him and yet unbearably aroused by his impatience. With a groan, Carlo lifted her and suckled at an erect pink nipple and her hands clenched fiercely into his shoulders, an involuntary moan of excitement torn from her. Her head fell back as his tormenting mouth bit at her sensitive flesh with a knowing eroticism that drove her out of her mind with excitement.

She was boneless in his grasp, a wanton creature drunk on sensation. A lean hand skimmed beneath the flimsy silken fabric of her gown, following the upward curve of a slender thigh and lingering there with devastating effect.

'You drive me crazy,' Carlo groaned, sinking to his knees to slowly tug down the scrap of lace that was all that divided him from her. 'You always drove me crazy.'

He buried his mouth hotly in the triangle of silver curls he had revealed and she started sliding down the wall until he gripped her thighs. 'No...' she mumbled in shock.

He didn't listen and a split-second later she stopped thinking altogether, thrown into a vortex of extraordinary excitement by what he was doing. She gasped his name, speared her fingers wildly into his tousled black hair and surrendered absolutely to the pleasure, losing all track of time.

When Carlo drew level with her again, she was inflamed to fever pitch, not a bone or a muscle in her body obedient to even the most confused command. He wound her arms round him and took her swollen mouth in a savage admission of need and then he lifted her, wrapping her thighs round his narrow waist and entered her in one compelling thrust.

Stilling, he shuddered against her, fighting for control. 'It's never been like this for me...*never*!' he rasped.

I love you... She found it on her lips and kept it there, instinct reining the confession back. Bracing her spine against the steel wall, he began to move again, fast and slow, smooth and rough until she was possessed by the primal rhythm and the explosive, uncontrollable hunger. As she reached an intolerable peak of excitement, she sank her teeth into his shoulder and was flung over the edge into quivering, whimpering fulfilment at the same time as he was.

His breathing pattern roughly audible, Carlo dealt her a shattered glance and slowly lowered her limp body to the floor again, glittering golden eyes still pinned to her. He dropped a kiss on to her brow and began rearranging her dress with hands that were uncharacteristically clumsy.

'We'd better get out of here.' He indicated the red light flashing behind the open control panel, readjusting whatever he had previously put out of place at speed. 'Security will be on their way.'

'What?' she moaned in horror.

The doors opened. Carlo grabbed her while she was still reeling incredulously from what she had allowed him to do. A few feet out of the lift, they were on to a staircase. Dear heaven, she acknowledged dazedly, that shameless woman in the lift had been her! She was pole-axed, barely functioning on automatic pilot.

Carlo dragged her into their bedroom, closed the door and slumped back against it. His narrowed gaze swept her hectically flushed features and then he burst out laughing. After a startled moment, she saw the humour of that indecently adolescent flight of theirs from authority and was overcome by helpless giggles.

'Like guilty teenagers!' Unselfconsciously, Carlo wiped at his damp eyes, fighting to rein back his laughter. 'I've never done anything like that in my life before.'

All threat of constraint banished, Jessica met his ruefully amused dark eyes and knew she had never loved him more than she loved him at that moment.

Abruptly, Carlo muttered an imprecation. 'I forgot about your poor feet.'

'I wasn't thinking about them,' she murmured shyly.

He took her into his bathroom and produced a medical kit. He made her sit on the edge of the bath and soak her feet. Then he crouched down and patted them dry with a fleecy towel. He was incredibly gentle and she watched him minister to her needs with growing astonishment. What a mixture of opposites he was, she thought painfully. The antiseptic he dabbed on stung like mad and tears sprang involuntarily to her eyes.

'You shouldn't swim for a couple of days.'

'Fine.'

Carlo swept her up and carried her back to the bedroom to deposit her on the bed. He sank down on the edge of the mattress and lifted the phone. 'Are you hungry?'

She discovered that she was. He ordered sandwiches.

As she stretched out, Carlo noticed the tear on her dress for the first time. Before she could object, he had peeled her out of it and discovered the angry scratch across her stomach. 'Please...not the antiseptic,' she begged in total cowardice.

Carlo grinned and pressed his lips tenderly to the abrasion, making her muscles clench suddenly tight with awareness. Lifting his dark head, he scrutinised her with sudden gravity. A tiny muscle pulsing at the corner of his compressed mouth. 'Last night,' he breathed. 'Last night when I saw that photograph of your late husband, I was insanely jealous.'

Entrapped by his dark eyes, she was shaken by his honesty.

'You knew,' he saw. 'I'm surprised you didn't throw it in my teeth.'

'In the mood you were in, I might just have ended up out in the corridor.'

'You chose him over me.' Carlo had shed his sense of humour and would not allow her to lightly flip the subject. 'That is why I felt jealous. If I had not known you then, he would merely be a part of your past.'

'I didn't choose——'

'You did ... you chose,' he asserted, allowing her no escape from that fact.

A knock on the door announced the arrival of supper. Jessica had rarely been so grateful for an interruption. Carlo collected the tray and settled it on the foot of the bed.

'I refuse to accept that I am second best,' Carlo continued tautly in the throbbing silence. 'For that is what you want me to accept ... I cannot do it.'

All relaxation banished, Jessica slid upright and reached for her robe.

'You say nothing,' he commented with flaring impatience.

'Maybe I don't want to fight with you——'

'No, you evade my every invitation for you to talk about your marriage. You close me out of five years of your life! You slam the door shut in my face——'

'I am not about to run Simon down just to please you,' Jessica muttered shakily.

'I do not expect that from you. I am not a child unable to face harsh realities. But I find your refusal to discuss Turner...peculiar,' Carlo selected, reaching for a sandwich, entirely at his ease. 'My life is now an open book to you——'

Her teeth gritted. 'Only because I stumbled accidentally between the covers.'

'I did not want my past to come between us,' Carlo stated levelly. 'You force me to be blunt. OK. Your father intimated that your marriage had not been a happy one.'

Taken by surprise, Jessica froze.

'And he was not talking about your husband's illness. He made that clear——'

'He had no right to imply that——'

'You were not blissfully happy with your *best friend*,' Carlo incised with scorn.

Jessica rolled off the bed, cornered by his persistence. 'I will not discuss Simon with you.'

'Why not? He is dead. He cannot be hurt.' Carlo dealt her an expectant stare.

'You say I made a choice. Why don't you look to your own behaviour during those six weeks?' she demanded. 'You might be surprised at what you see!'

'I behaved like a bastard,' Carlo growled the admission to her back a second before she vanished into the bathroom. 'But you didn't encourage me to be anything else. You made me angry and frustrated and you challenged me. You made it an all-out fight between us and I know only one way to fight...and that is to win!'

She ran a bath for herself. She needed the space. In full flood, Carlo was a talented interrogator. The water stung her feet like mad but a masochistic part of her rejoiced in the pain. She deserved it. She kept on letting her guard down around Carlo and manipulative swine that he was, he sensed that every time it happened and demanded answers he had no right to expect.

Once, she had been grossly disloyal to Simon with Carlo. Ultimately that hadn't mattered, except in so far as she had contravened her own high principles. But she could not be disloyal to Simon's memory. How could she tell a male as rawly virile and passionate as Carlo that Simon had failed to consummate their marriage? He would laugh, wouldn't he? He would kill himself laughing. He would be triumphant, possessed of the knowledge that her marriage had been pure farce from start to finish and that he, after all, had become her first lover. She felt that she owed Simon's memory something more than that.

She emerged to an empty bedroom and instead of being relieved felt deserted. Furious at her own increasing emotional dependency on Carlo, she compressed her lips. She could not afford to look for Carlo when he was not there. Some day not too far in the future, he would not be there at all.

Unintentionally, she recalled the passion they had shared and reddened fiercely, still barely able to credit that that wanton woman had been her. Carlo touched her and that was that. Nothing else mattered. Sooner or later, she would pay a heavy price for such memories, she acknowledged painfully. The fact that Carlo had finally contrived to fulfil his fantasy of having sex in a lift was unlikely to be a recollection she cherished with pride...when he was gone.

'Some day you will come to me on your knees and beg me to take you...and I will break you.' Jessica shivered, suddenly cold and scared. Just a few short days ago, Carlo had still been talking in the same vein. And though he had yet to discover it, he had already won. She loved him. Whatever happened, she was going to be very badly hurt.

Another knock sounded on the door. It was fresh sandwiches and sweetly fragrant coffee, ordered by Carlo on her behalf. The pretty dark-skinned maid passed on the message that Carlo was with his father.

'I'm sorry you had to be bothered so late.' It was two in the morning and Jessica felt guilty.

'But I work the night shift here, ma'am.' The woman smiled. 'This is my job.'

The night shift, Jessica reflected, slowly shaking her head. A night shift of staff for round-the-clock service. It was like living in a top-flight hotel. Then she wondered if Lukas had taken a turn for the worse and frowned.

Carlo returned about ten minutes later. 'How is Lukas?' she asked.

'A consummate insomniac,' Carlo sighed. 'Problems have arisen over a shipping deal in Athens. He's asked me to fly out there and take care of them. I'll be leaving at seven and I expect to be back the night before the wedding.'

Disappointment enveloped her and she fought to conceal it.

'You'll miss me,' Carlo asserted with teeth-clenching conviction.

He slid into bed beside her and tugged her into his arms with determination. His lean, muscular frame felt surprisingly tense. 'Something occurred to me earlier.' He lifted his head. 'Are you on the Pill?'

It was Jessica's turn to tense. 'No.'

Carlo expelled his breath in a hiss. 'I didn't protect you this time...I'm sorry.'

She flushed, made some feverish calculations and decided that the risk of pregnancy was so small as to be most unlikely. 'There isn't very much chance——'

'Russian roulette,' Carlo groaned. 'I have never been that careless.'

Jessica was stiffening. 'I really don't think you have anything to worry about.'

It would be very foolish to forget the true parameters of their relationship, she appreciated. Passion had intervened to blur those limits but there was something horribly realistic about Carlo's alarm at the prospect of repercussions.

'We'll see.' Carlo looked fatalistic and shrugged a smooth brown shoulder. 'Perhaps it is just as well that we will be getting married.'

'It won't be a real marriage.'

'What is real and what unreal?' Carlo murmured wryly above her downbent head. 'I am not sure I know any more.'

'I thought you knew everything——'

'I have moments of occasional insanity——'

'In lifts?' The quip flew off her tongue, embarrassing her.

'Only with you,' Carlo muttered with earthy amusement, splaying a determined hand across her bottom and bringing her into closer connection with his highly aroused body. Her eyes widened in shock at his readiness to make love again. It occurred to her that she was at the very foot of the learning curve in this particular field.

Carlo surveyed her with unhidden satisfaction. 'You really are the most gloriously passionate woman…I find you irresistible.'

Sexually, not intellectually, she affixed, rather bitterly aware that a fortnight ago she would have wanted to hit him for looking at her with that air of arrogant ownership but now she was busy drowning in dark golden eyes and longing for the heat of that expert mouth on hers. Her mother had spoken with the wisdom of a seer six years ago. This time she really had fallen flat on her face.

* * *

'You look ravishing.' Surveying Jessica, Marika sighed with heartfelt satisfaction. 'My brother will worship at your feet.'

Jessica tautened. She could not imagine Carlo worshipping her. Carlo's instincts were far more basic, but then his sister was a hopeless romantic. Jessica attempted to scan her reflection without being gripped by any similar fantasies. She wouldn't have objected to wearing a smart suit. But she had not envisaged wearing anything that remotely resembled a wedding-dress.

And here she was, sheathed in the most devastatingly bridal concoction she had ever seen. Sizzling white with a superb beaded Elizabethan collar, the whole covered with magnificent embroidery and even sweeping down into a small train. Her mistake had been protesting the unsuitability of such a gown within Lukas's hearing. She had never dreamt he would even interest himself in what she wore.

'All my wives wore white,' Lukas had interrupted loudly. 'It's part of the show——'

'But I'm a widow——'

'A merry one?' Lukas had chuckled with great amusement at his own timeworn joke. 'We don't advertise these things. You wear white.'

Recalling her intense mortification, she began to peel off the dress. Marika handled it with reverence, turning to a hovering maid for assistance lest the smallest damage be done to the delicate fabric. As Carlo's sister left to dress for dinner, Jessica realised that in less than twenty-four hours she would be married. Married to the man she loved but who did not love her, married as part of a deal to please a dying old man. It was crazy...why had she allowed Carlo to persuade her to play along?

Jessica was putting the finishing touches to her make-up when the door opened without warning. Sunny strolled in, clad in a glistening grey sheath dress. Jessica hadn't laid eyes on Sunny for over forty-eight hours, not since seeing her with Carlo. Over breakfast the next morning, Marika had informed her that Sunny had flown to Miami on one of her regular shopping trips.

'Do you want something?' she asked drily, infuriated by the fashion in which Sunny simply walked in without knocking.

Green eyes glittered coldly over her. Sunny uttered a brittle laugh. 'All of a sudden you're very sure of yourself, aren't you?'

Jessica looked back at her, refusing to be discomfited. Calmly, she stood up and crossed the room to slide her feet into shoes but behind the cool front, her nervous tension was running at an all-time high. Physically Sunny had an impact that took even Jessica's breath away. Carlo was undeniably aware of this woman's beauty. Could he really be quite untouched by her desire for him?

'You saw us together the other night,' Sunny murmured with faintly patronising amusement. 'Didn't that bother you at all?'

With a not quite steady hand, Jessica lifted a silver-backed brush that belonged to Carlo from the dressing-table and ran it through her hair slowly. 'I saw nothing that bothered me,' she lied.

'You're in love with him too, aren't you? Poor Jessica. I can imagine what he's told you. I can also imagine just how much you wanted to believe him——'

Jessica took a deep breath. 'If you don't mind, I'd like to finish getting ready.'

'If you don't mind...you're so polite!' Sunny scanned her with wide, wondering eyes. 'He won't have told you the truth. The truth is that *neither* of us matters a damn to him right now. Carlo's one priority is keeping his darling daddy happy.'

'Why shouldn't it be?' Jessica said defensively. 'He hasn't got much time left with him.'

'And his inheritance is conditional on his marriage...did you know that?' Sunny prompted gently.

'Right now, Carlo has to play you along and keep you happy. He needs a bride and it seems he's found one, dumb enough to shut her eyes to reality.'

The floor rocked under Jessica's feet. She turned pale. 'I don't believe you,' she said shakily.

'You are naïve... and you haven't a clue how the men in this family operate.' Sunny's exquisite face twisted with derisive amusement. 'I understand Carlo. You don't understand him at all. Carlo wants me and he fully intends to have me... but he won't put a foot wrong while his father is still alive. All that keeps Carlo from me now is Lukas... and of course, the money...'

As the door shut on Sunny's exit Jessica closed her eyes tightly in anguish. She felt physically sick. Carlo had lied to her. He was not marrying her purely to please his father. He was marrying her for entirely mercenary motives. And yet he had fooled her brilliantly into believing everything he had told her!

In a wild passion of despair and turmoil, Jessica hauled her cases out of a closet in the dressing-room and began dragging her clothes out and packing them. She refused to be used like that... she absolutely refused!

'What the hell are you doing?'

On her knees beside the cases, Jessica glanced up. Carlo was a big dark silhouette filling the doorway. Hooded ebony eyes dug into her like aggressive question marks as he stared down at her in disbelief.

'I'm not going through with the wedding!' she gasped.

CHAPTER NINE

CARLO scanned the wildness in her amethyst eyes for a fulminating ten seconds, a muscle jerking tight at his hard jawline. 'I don't know what the hell you think you're playing at but the wedding goes ahead tomorrow...even if I have to drag you through it by the hair!'

'No. Sunny told me why you *had* to get married!' Jessica slung rawly. 'And I refuse to be part of it!'

'Why do I have to get married?' Carlo invited very softly. 'I really would like to know.'

'You lied to me,' Jessica condemned fiercely. 'Everything you told me was a lie...you played on my sympathy when all the time you were just using me——'

'Do you ever get to the punchline?'

'You *have* to be married to inherit your father's money!'

After a staggered pause, Carlo threw back his dark imperious head and laughed uproariously, utterly incredulous at the charge.

It was not the reaction Jessica had expected. Her mouth fell open.

'*Dio*...is that the best she could do?' His amusement spent, Carlo studied Jessica with narrowed eyes, his hard mouth compressing. 'And you believed her, didn't you?'

Suddenly less sure, Jessica said, 'I——'

Carlo cut across her. 'I have been my father's heir since the day I was born because his blood runs in my veins. And no matter what bitterness or resentment lay

144

between us that has never changed. Why would he demand that I marry?'

'Because he wants you to settle down,' Jessica suggested tremulously.

'Lukas Philippides wants me to do what he never did himself?' Carlo elevated a sardonic winged brow. 'Settle down? He didn't settle down through four marriages and countless mistresses ... why should he seek to interfere in my private life?'

Jessica was not prepared to cede the point without a fight. 'Well, then, you tell me why both your father and your sister are so damned glad that you're getting married?' she demanded, shooting what she knew to be the last bolt in her argument.

His hard features perceptibly darkened, his mouth tightening as though she had drawn blood. Glittering golden eyes rested on her coldly. 'OK, I'll tell you. Ten years ago, my father went to bed with the woman I had asked to marry me——'

'He *what*?' Jessica mumbled in shock, certain she could not have heard him correctly.

'Thus a decade of mutual silence,' Carlo pointed out grimly.

'But how ... I mean, *why*?' she whispered.

'Lukas invited me to visit him. I brought my fiancée with me,' Carlo murmured in a flat, unemotional tone. 'You see Lukas now, a shadow of the man he was then. In those days he was still virile and attractive to women. He wanted me to work for him. That was why the red carpet came out. My half-brother was a drunk, useless in business. Lukas wanted me back to take his place. I refused. I knew it wouldn't work. He was furious and Bella was furious too. She loved the lifestyle he was offering ... the constant parties, the bottomless well of money. I wasn't one quarter as wealthy then as I am now——'

'But still——' Jessica found herself still arguing her own disbelief, she was so shattered by the very idea of what he was telling her.

'Lukas made a play for Bella. She was flattered and he took her to bed——'

Jessica was appalled. Dear God, he had been twenty-three years old! How could any father have done that to his own son and how could any woman sink that low?

'I found them together,' Carlo volunteered in the dragging silence. 'And I was devastated. I knew *he* couldn't be trusted with any beautiful woman but I had assumed that I could trust *her*——'

'How could they do that to you?' Jessica felt physically sick.

'Lukas can't help competing and he doesn't always think ahead. He was settling old scores, showing the young dog that the old dog still had a trick or two up his sleeve. Bella?' Carlo's mouth compressed. 'One of the wealthiest men in the world told her he wanted her and she was knocked sideways by the idea. She was dumb enough to think he would marry her but he dumped her a couple of weeks later. He knew he'd gone too far——'

'But how could you ever forgive him?'

'Because he doesn't know any better. Like a bull in a china shop, he creates havoc and lets other people pay the price, but ultimately, he's still my father.' Carlo surveyed her pale, troubled face. 'Now you know why my father and my sister are so damned glad I'm getting married,' he derided harshly. 'It buries that tacky little episode with Bella.'

Jessica was still in shock, stricken by an awareness of the pain that must have been inflicted by a cheap little gold-digger who had her eye on a richer quarry. Carlo was so proud and at that age he must have been far more vulnerable.

'You were so quick to accept the word of a most unreliable character witness...incredibly quick,' Carlo condemned her now with contempt. 'Sunny is jealous and will do just about anything to cause trouble between us. Didn't that occur to you?'

She hadn't taken time to think. She had acted on impulse. Now her loss of faith in him seemed heinous. Her cheeks flamed. 'I'm sorry...'

'I really believed I was getting somewhere with you,' Carlo breathed harshly. 'And I was wrong. I open my heart to you and you still kick me in the teeth. You have no faith, no trust to give. As far as you're concerned, I'm still the bastard you decided I was six years ago and as far as I'm concerned I might as well be from now on!'

Her throat was convulsing. There was a pain in his dark, clenched features that she had never seen before. It cut her up inside. 'I said I was sorry! It's this situation——'

Carlo swung on his heel, unmoved by her unhidden distress. 'Your father's waiting downstairs for you——'

'My father?' she echoed weakly.

'I picked him up on the way through London. I thought you would want him here.'

She swallowed hard. 'I——'

'You'd better tidy yourself up before dinner,' Carlo cut her off with bite.

Why *had* she listened to Sunny? In retrospect, it seemed very foolish of her to have placed credence in anything the other woman said. Sunny was not reliable. Sunny had set her sights on Carlo and she was jealous. Jessica covered her face with shaking hands. And she herself was inclined to be jealous of Sunny, she acknowledged. Had it been easier to latch on to the accusation about his inheritance than confront him with

Sunny's confident belief that only filial loyalty prevented Carlo from admitting that he *did* want his father's wife? Sunny had been horribly convincing.

But Carlo was right. She didn't trust him. No faith, no trust. Had Simon done that to her as well? She had trusted Simon from childhood and he had let her down badly by using her, uncaring of how much he might hurt her. He had been too weak to care and he had depended on her loyalty and her pride to keep her quiet and carry on the pretence of their marriage. Suddenly she knew that she owed Carlo that truth, no matter how distressing she found sharing it.

In the bedroom, Carlo was halfway into a shirt, muscles flexed across his smooth brown back as he shrugged into it, and her mouth ran dry. 'Carlo...' she whispered. 'I think I should tell you about my marriage——'

'You can keep him like some holy icon inside your heart.' He spun round and sent her a chilling glance of impassivity. 'I'm not competing with a ghost——'

'You wouldn't be competing——'

'You don't understand,' Carlo breathed with cold dark eyes that froze her out. 'Simon's the past and as irrelevant as yesterday's newspaper to me. What is important is trust and you haven't got any to give. You hadn't any six years ago either!'

'Don't throw that up to me now. You said you'd never forgive me on the way over here,' she reminded him shakily. 'That does not create an atmosphere of trust.'

'I'll see you downstairs.' Carlo snatched up his dinner-jacket and strode to the door. 'You'd better wash your face. Your mascara's running.'

Jessica smacked her coiled fist against the wall in frustration as the door slammed and then curved the injured member into her stomach, wincing with pain. Sometimes, Carlo was so hatefully superior that she wanted to hit him! Loving him didn't wipe out that temptation. And now he had brought her father over as if this were a normal wedding. Dazedly she shook her head.

Gerald Amory was chatting animatedly to Marika when she entered the drawing-room and Jessica barely had time to kiss his cheek before Lukas arrived and her father was taken over. Throughout dinner, Carlo's father shot questions at her father, demanding his opinions on business practices and frequently censuring them. Gerald Amory stood up to the interrogation well, wry amusement in his gaze when he caught Jessica's anxious look.

'Well, I wouldn't employ you,' Lukas grumbled over his coffee. 'I don't believe in feather-bedding my workers——'

'The EC rulings won't give you much choice,' Gerald Amory dared.

After dinner, she was left alone with her father.

'Am I to believe you've finally taken leave of your wits?' he teased. 'I never thought I'd see the day that you did anything at reckless speed and here you are rushing into marriage within weeks of meeting Carlo again!'

Jessica tensed. 'What did he tell you?'

'Oh he was very persuasive,' Gerald laughed. 'Never shut up about you the whole flight!'

'Really?' Jessica encouraged.

'Told me he fell in love with you at first sight six years ago and never recovered. Very impressive stuff, it was,' her father recalled with a fond smile. 'He did explain that his father's condition was pressing you both into a quick marriage but he stressed that he could have married you a couple of weeks ago just as happily!' he chuckled.

Her strained smile glazed over. Dear heaven, Carlo had laid on the I-love-your-daughter routine with a trowel. Very impressive indeed.

'Carlo's a rather more complex character than I ever appreciated,' Gerald admitted. 'I always thought of him as very cool and controlled. He is in business. But in love...he's all emotion and reaction. So, now you tell me how you feel.'

Jessica took a deep breath. 'I'm crazy about him.'

'And you're much more reserved than he is...did your mother and I do that to you?' he sighed regretfully.

She went to bed about eleven. There was no sign of Carlo. She lay sleepless in the darkness waiting for him. But he didn't come and she was hurt. Why was it that when she finally decided to open *her* heart, Carlo closed her out? It was impossible to believe that tomorrow was her wedding-day. But then it wasn't a real wedding-day, she reminded herself wretchedly.

The next morning she was served breakfast in bed. There was an air of strong excitement in the household and from dawn overhead the ceaseless racket of rotor blades as guests were flown in for the festivities.

It was to be a very small wedding, Marika had explained. Just relatives, her father's closest business associates and executive staff and of course Carlo's friends. It was rather sad that she listed not one single person as a friend of her father's. Like someone in a dream, Jessica let herself be fussed over and dressed. She was merely playing a part, she told herself repeatedly, just going through the expected motions to please everybody.

'It's time,' Marika said from the door with a misty smile.

'Their idea of a small do wouldn't be ours,' her father shared out of the corner of his mouth on their passage down the huge main staircase. All the staff were in the main hall to see her.

And a minute later, as the music sounded up and she had a startled glimpse of the hundreds of people packed into the vast ballroom with standing room only at the back, she understood what he meant. Every head seemed to turn, a rippling sigh of comment accompanying their passing. Her pallor was banished by colour as Carlo swung round impatiently to unsmilingly watch her approach. Like the condemned man, she thought furiously, on the brink of being forced to walk the plank!

The ceremony seemed endless and it was conducted in both Greek and English. Carlo slotted the ring on her finger with a cool, steady hand. And it was done. He was not invited to kiss the bride and, although the opportunity came as she turned to face him, he took no advantage of it. His darkly handsome features were starkly set.

Her throat tightening, she glanced away and caught a no more cheering view of Lukas beaming with satisfaction and Sunny beside him, her stunning face wearing a set smile.

'Well, I'm glad that farce is over,' Jessica hissed before they made their exit.

Carlo swung her round like a doll and brought his mouth crashing down on hers in punishment, his powerful hands biting painfully into her wrists. She knew he was furious. She knew she wasn't supposed to enjoy it. But her body had other ideas. It went into instant meltdown like he had thrown a self-destruct button.

'No farce,' Carlo murmured softly, nastily as he lifted his dark head again and smiled for the assembled audience. 'You are my wife now, legally, morally and in every other way.'

There were no speeches over the banquet which followed. Lukas, she was informed by her father, didn't like speeches. Many toasts were offered and made. Jessica began to notice that Carlo's attention was frequently directed at Sunny. He did it cleverly, covertly, but he did all the same, she noted painfully.

Sunny, ravishing in silver and gold, her bright hair an eyecatching beacon every time she moved her head. 'Titian hair...my besetting sin,' Carlo had once confided. Jessica's stomach clenched. Why did she have to remember that now? An hour ago, Sunny had looked frozen, but now she was effervescent and glowing like a blazing torch.

After the meal, Carlo whirled her on to the empty floor while everybody sat back and watched. Jessica was desperately self-conscious. She had never danced with him before and was suddenly tortured by the lack of such small experiences in their relationship. They had never had a courtship, never dated and yet she loved him with a passion that burned and flamed more with every increasingly insecure moment.

'When are you going to start talking to me again?' she whispered.

'Have I stopped? You mean I might actually have something to say that you might want to hear?'

'I said I was sorry...what do you want me to do? Crawl?'

'I think I might enjoy that,' Carlo admitted.

'Well, I'm not about to do it...dream on!'

As he bound her closer, she felt his breath on her cheek and clashed with smouldering golden eyes and an explicitly sexual scrutiny. 'If you want me in your bed tonight, you'll have to do better than that——'

Her skin flamed scarlet and she trembled, cursing her innate and inescapable physical awareness of him. He could feel it. She knew that. 'I can do without you in my bed.'

He laughed huskily. 'You're as much a slave to the passion as I am!'

But I want more; I want it all, a little voice screamed inside her head.

'I counted the hours I was away from you,' Carlo suddenly groaned above her head. 'And then I found you packing——'

She missed a step but he carried her on effortlessly. Through the light fabric of her gown, she could feel the thrust of his arousal and her knees went weak, her breath feathering dangerously short in her dry throat. Her nipples were tight little points that ached under the tight bodice. 'I'm sorry...'

'I'm getting more forgiving by the second,' Carlo gritted, binding her even closer so that she was in contact with every inch of his powerful body.

She was trembling by the time they came off the floor but radiant. Lukas beckoned to her as Carlo dropped her hand. Her father-in-law indicated that he wanted her to bend her head. 'What would you say if I told you I wasn't leaving him a *drachma*?'

Still radiant, she laughed. 'I'd say he doesn't need your money.'

'You love him. Make him happy. That's all I want,' Lukas growled.

Across the room, Sunny was the centre of a crowd of bedazzled men. Jessica saw Carlo several yards away and his hooded dark eyes were trained on Sunny. Suddenly sick, Jessica looked away. Lukas had already moved on but Marika appeared at her elbow.

'Men find Sunny quite irresistible, don't they?' Jessica remarked helplessly.

'Men like my father,' Marika conceded wryly. 'She's an expensive adornment, other men envy. That's why Lukas married her when his health was failing. He gets to show her off; she gets to spend the money. And I have to admit that in recent months she's surprised me——'

'How?'

'She's been leading a very restricted life here on Paradiso and she's handled it better than I expected,' Marika conceded. 'Then she knows her freedom is on the horizon, and Sunny isn't the kind of woman likely to be on her own for long. Right now, she's probably looking out for her next meal ticket and I can't really blame her. Lukas forced her to sign a pre-nuptial contract. When he dies, she gets next to nothing.'

Marika clearly had no idea that Sunny had already targeted Lukas's replacement and that she was keeping it in the family, so as to speak. Only Jessica had got in her way.

Carlo's sister sighed, still watching Sunny flirting like mad with her admirers. 'I wonder why she's upset today.'

'Upset?' Sunny looked anything but upset to Jessica's untutored gaze. The redhead appeared to be revelling in all the attention she was receiving.

'Something's bothering her. She's drinking too much,' Marika proffered. 'She knows how my father feels about that. She's usually more careful.'

Carlo crossed the room with a brilliant smile that tore at Jessica's heartstrings. 'What are you doing over here? Come on . . . I want you to meet my friends.'

The afternoon wore on and the party became more riotous. Jessica didn't know what time it was when she overheard Marika say something to Carlo in Greek. She caught Sunny's name and Carlo's sudden tension. His hard jawline squared.

Where was Sunny? It had been some time since Jessica had last seen her. A split-second later, Carlo strode off.

'Where's he going?' she asked his sister.

Marika compressed her lips. 'I asked him to find Sunny. She's drunk and when she's drunk, she can be . . . indiscreet,' she selected the word curtly.

Jessica hesitated only a moment before setting off in pursuit. She saw Carlo at the top of the stairs and hurried after him. He clearly knew exactly where he was going and she almost lost him down one corridor, catching up round a corner just in time to see him throw wide a door.

Before she saw for herself the scene that had met his eyes, she heard him explode into guttural Greek. Sunny was half out of her dress on a bed and a highly embarrassed young man was spluttering fervent apologies and struggling to get back into his jacket beside the bed. Carlo stood there with clenched fists, a dark flush highlighting his blazing eyes.

'You don't want me,' Sunny slurred, fumbling clumsily to right her dress. 'Why should you care?'

As the young man took advantage of Carlo's stasis to flee, Jessica was almost knocked flying. Her gasp as she grabbed at the door-handle to steady herself turned both Carlo and Sunny's heads.

Sunny gave an inebriated giggle. 'If it isn't the blushing bride...come on, why don't you? It's open house!'

Carlo was rigid, his dark, strong face utterly impassive. 'Go back downstairs, Jessica.'

'She's not that sensitive.' Sunny laughed again. 'I know all about her, Carlo. I found the file in Lukas's desk. Her mother was a nymphomaniac and her daddy's a thief. You weren't too choosy, were you?'

'Shut up!' Carlo gritted furiously as every scrap of colour drained from Jessica's shattered face.

'And her first husband was gay,' Sunny giggled, unconcerned. 'You must be a real shock to the old system after an experience like that!'

Carlo stilled. His fiercely narrowed gaze slewed at speed back to Jessica and simply stayed there. 'Gay?' he practically whispered in disbelief.

Jessica unfroze and whirled out of the room. She was outraged and devastated at one and the same time. Lukas Philippides must have had her investigated. Where else could Sunny have obtained such information? All along

Lukas had known about her background. She felt invaded and violated, horrified that such information should have fallen into Sunny's grasping hands, cheap fodder for her spite.

Carlo caught her back on the landing before she could head for the sanctuary of their bedroom. A far from gentle hand closed round her forearm. 'Pull yourself together!' he warned her with barely subdued ferocity.

He wasn't laughing. He looked furious, rage threatening to seethe up through the cracks. Jessica felt torn in two. Last night, she had wanted to tell Carlo the story of her marriage and he had denied her the opportunity. She was humiliated by the manner in which Sunny had deprived her of that right.

Carlo's hands curved powerfully into her shoulders. His dark face pale and set. 'Is it true?' he demanded.

'None of your blasted business!' she gasped. 'Why don't you go ask Sunny for the same sleazy invasion of my life and read it for yourself?'

'I might just do that.' Carlo released her with pronounced reluctance and bit out, '*Dio* ... if it is true, I don't think I'll be responsible for my actions!'

He made her rejoin the party, his arm an iron vice clamped to her rigid spine. He held her so close she could feel the tremors of repressed rage still shuddering through him. 'Smile,' he instructed harshly.

Later she remembered nothing of the last couple of hours of the wedding. Did she smile? She could not understand why Carlo should be so angry. Surely the right to anger was hers alone? It was her privacy which had been crudely and shockingly invaded. A nymphomaniac, Sunny had called her mother. That more than anything else made Jessica feel physically sick with humiliation.

'To think I thought the impossibility of a honeymoon unfortunate,' Carlo drawled in a murderously quiet tone as he flung off his jacket and tie. 'In these circumstances, it would have been grotesque!'

Jessica was stationed by the window, her slender back defensively turned to him.

'You're like Pandora's box...what else don't I know?' Carlo enquired with flat emphasis.

'I wasn't the only one who kept secrets,' she reminded him tautly. 'Just when were you going to tell me that Sunny was after you?'

'That was different.'

'How dare your father have me investigated?' Jessica suddenly gasped with renewed outrage.

Carlo released his breath in a hiss. 'I should have expected that——'

'Is that all you've got to say about it?' Jessica demanded hotly.

'It's done now,' Carlo pointed out drily. 'And I wish I had done it myself——'

Jessica turned in disbelief. 'I beg your pardon?'

'I will request that he has it destroyed. His security must be getting very lax if Sunny was able to get her hands on his private papers.' Carlo shot her pale face a look of grim challenge. 'So now you start at the beginning and tell me everything.'

She stiffened, antagonism leaping through her. 'Last night you weren't interested——'

'Last night I had no idea what you were hiding.'

'I hid nothing. My marriage was my business.'

Carlo dealt her a seething stare, an antagonism equal to her own firing the atmosphere. 'Six years ago, you made it mine.'

She went rigid but she held her head high. 'When I told Simon what had happened between us, he said that it didn't matter to him——'

'He said what?' Carlo broke in incredulously.

Her throat closed over, her voice emerging unevenly. 'I wanted to cancel the wedding. He begged me not to. He told me that he needed me...couldn't imagine life without me. He said he forgave me absolutely,' she recited with a quivering lower lip, 'and that there was no reason for me to ruin our future just because of one silly mistake.'

'And you swallowed that...*Dio*!' Carlo framed with gathering temper, spreading his hands wide as if to appeal for some shred of sanity from her.

Hot moisture smarted behind her eyes. 'I thought that he loved me enough to forgive me and I didn't want to let him down——'

'You married him because you felt sorry for him!' Carlo stabbed back at her.

'I felt safe with him. I thought he cared. I really thought we could be happy!' she returned with feverish emphasis. 'Our relationship had never been based on sex. What happened with you...it frightened me, and the way you reacted afterwards——'

'Go ahead, blame it all on me!' Carlo slashed back ferociously.

Jessica spun back to the window before the tears could fall. 'What I did with you,' she repeated shakily, 'well, it was the sort of thing my mother would have done, and in the Deangate Hotel of all places, which *she* used to haunt. It was my worst nightmare come true. I behaved like her and it terrified me——'

'I hardly touched you!' Carlo cut in ruthlessly.

'That didn't change how I felt. It was the fact that I lost control that was scary, the fact that I wanted you to make love to me,' she admitted brokenly.

'I want to hear about your marriage,' Carlo told her rawly.

Jessica drew in a deep shuddering breath of air. 'Simon got very drunk on our wedding-night. And every night after it. I thought it was my fault . . . that he just couldn't bring himself to touch me because of you. And he let me think that . . . he let me think that for so long!' she gasped painfully. 'It was hell. We didn't even share a bedroom when we came home and when I tried to talk to him about it he walked out and stayed away . . .'

Carlo uttered a ground-out imprecation and she shivered.

'He wouldn't go to marriage guidance or anything. He refused to admit that there was a problem . . .'

'Why the hell didn't you leave him?' Carlo roared at her.

A sob caught in her throat. 'Guilt. I did think it was my fault. It wasn't until he became ill that he admitted that he was impotent . . . and that he had never wanted any woman physically,' she recounted jerkily. 'Some people just don't have a sex drive and I believe that Simon was one of them. I don't think he was gay but apparently, before he asked me to get engaged, there had been rumours about him. He was terrified of his family and friends thinking that he was gay . . . that's why he married me. He used me to hide behind. It stopped people wondering——'

'And this is the bastard you called your best friend?' Carlo murmured tautly.

A choked laugh escaped her. She was shaking. Remembering brought all the pain and suffering back. 'He was until I married him,' she muttered with unconcealed bitterness.

'Did you ever consider walking out?'

'Not once he was ill,' she whispered. 'I felt cheated but I felt I'd asked for what I got——'

'You owed him nothing. He knew about me before he married you. You gave him a free choice. What choice did he give you?'

She wiped shakily at her overflowing eyes. 'None,' she conceded.

'He lied by omission. He deceived you. Why do you still seek to defend him at your own expense?' She was stunned when she felt his arms close round her. Momentarily she went rigid. Carlo drew her firmly back into the hard heat of his powerful body. 'Don't cry...I can't bear it when you cry,' he said roughly.

'I thought I loved him,' she mumbled fiercely. 'I grew up thinking I loved him and I would have trusted him with my life. Not much of a judge of character, was I?'

'You were very young and I was arrogant,' Carlo breathed. 'I never once thought of how you must have felt that day. I couldn't believe that you would still marry him. You said that I never thought of the damage I was causing...you were right. I only thought of winning.'

'Why are you being so understanding?'

Turning her round, he studied her with intent golden eyes that glittered with all-male satisfaction. 'It takes an accomplished liar to recall her lies,' he murmured with fierce amusement. 'Four days ago you lied to me after I made love to you...why did you lie?'

Too late, she remembered her denial of her own inexperience. Her pallor was put to flight by hot colour.

'You were a virgin. Why pretend otherwise?'

'I felt I owed that to Simon's memory,' she whispered, stiff with mortification.

'And maybe you didn't want to give me the pleasure of knowing that I was the first,' Carlo completed shrewdly, but he smiled none the less.

The one lie she could tell Carlo and be magnificently, generously forgiven for, she realised dazedly. Why had she ever thought he would laugh when she told him about her unconsummated marriage?

The joy of conquest had just been made all the sweeter for Carlo. On that level, Carlo was primitive. She understood him perfectly. She had never belonged to any other man in the physical sense. On Carlo's terms that meant she belonged that much more to him. All jealousy was magically banished. Simon had not, after all, managed to *take* what Carlo had regarded as his by right six years ago.

'Let's go down to the beach,' Carlo suggested softly.

In bemusement she blinked. 'The beach?'

'This house suffocates me.'

A rueful grin slowly tilted her mouth. 'You want me to go down to the beach got up like this?'

Carlo flipped her round and suggestively ran down the zip.

Breathlessly she tugged a shocking pink sundress from the closet and slid her feet into flatties. She felt extra-ordinarily carefree as she walked out on to the terrace to join him. Carlo had changed into jeans and removed the bottle of champagne from the ice bucket beside the bed.

He dropped an arm round her bare shoulders. 'Come on.'

'What did you do with that shoe I left behind six years ago?' she heard herself ask. She had always wondered.

'It's about somewhere.'

'Oh.'

'Did you think I might have had it dipped in pure gold and placed in a glass case?' he teased.

'It was one of my favourite shoes.'

'What did you do with the one you had left?'

'Dumped it.'

'There you are, then,' Carlo mocked. 'I was more sentimental than you were.'

'I thought you'd laugh about Simon.'

'Why? It wasn't funny. He put you through a lot of pain and you didn't deserve that. I'm not a sadist. Although two weeks ago I was outraged by the idea that you had been blissfully happy with him. A lot can change in two weeks...'

'Yes,' she conceded, her voice a whisper of sound.

'Although I'm still desperate to know how you define a "travelling tart"!' he confided.

'You offered me a life of luxury on the move in return for sex!' she snapped.

'I couldn't stay in England forever. I wanted you to myself. What was wrong with that? We hardly knew each other. I didn't know whether or not the attraction between us would last. I was honest with you——'

'You were an ignorant, egocentric swine!' Jessica returned with spirit.

Carlo shifted a broad shoulder. 'Possibly I could have wrapped it up a little more tactfully but I was angry with you and uncertain of my own feelings. Once bitten, twice shy... after Bella,' he admitted drily. 'I didn't want to make another mistake. I wasn't going to make promises I might not keep. It never at any stage crossed my mind that you might still marry Simon. I thought *that* was over from the moment you melted in my arms... and if he had been any other man it would have been.'

'Did you love her very much?' she couldn't prevent herself from asking.

'Who?'

'Bella!'

'At the time, I believed I did. Now I think she might just have been a trophy on my arm. Like Sunny, she was stunningly eye-catching,' Carlo mused softly. 'Lukas always went for women like that, the kind of women other men would kill to have. What was underneath didn't count. Maybe that's why I chose Bella... maybe in my own way I was competing too. I was a lot more like Lukas then than I like to admit.'

'Like Sunny, she was stunningly eye-catching...' He said it so carelessly. He did not deny the strength of

Sunny's physical appeal. Jessica endured a fresh stab of insecurity. She recalled Carlo's blazing fury when he found the redhead with that young man...and Sunny's almost taunting amusement. Then she told herself off. Carlo had given her no cause to distrust him and she was being foolish.

'Were you shocked by what——?' she began.

Carlo stilled and pulled her close. 'Shut up,' he said softly. 'I want to kiss you.'

Helplessly, she smiled. 'You don't usually ask in advance.'

He splayed a masterful hand over the rounded swell of her hips and pressed her into the hard heat of his lean thighs. 'Fate had it in for me when it served you up six years ago.'

The scent and the feel of him made her tremble. And when it came, it was the most devastating kiss. It stole the soul from her body and rocked her from her head to her toes. He released her reddened lips slowly and stared down at her, glittering dark eyes sweeping her rapt face with satisfaction.

They walked along the beach in a curiously peaceful silence. It was a gorgeous night. She kicked off her shoes and walked into the surf whispering on to the shore. The water was warm but cool on her hot feet, gloriously soothing to toes cooped up in stilettos all day.

'Come here,' Carlo said thickly.

She turned with quicksilver grace and looked across at him and the simple pleasure of the water was forgotten. She looked...and she ached with a need that ran far deeper than desire. Her feet carried her back as though he had yanked a string. It was an irresistible pull. He reached for her and she was boneless with anticipation, adrenalin racing through her veins, heat surging between her thighs. For the very first time, she rejoiced in her own response, neither unnerved by nor ashamed of it.

In fact, she drowned in the meeting of their mouths as desperate as he was for that fierce contact. In the midst of it he shed his shirt; she wriggled feverishly out of her dress. Her breasts felt heavy, swollen, and a soft gasp was torn from her throat as he discovered for himself that she had not bothered to wear a bra. He groaned his approval, shaping her aching flesh with hungry hands, his thumbs glancing over her painfully aroused nipples before he crushed her against his hair-roughened chest.

He shuddered and lifted his head. 'Every time I touch you, I want you more than I did the last time... but this time I want to go slow——'

'Next time.' Reaching up, she framed his hard cheek-bones with loving fingertips and drew him back down to her again, incredibly hungry for the scorching heat of his mouth. Daringly, she employed a tactic he had taught her. She ran the tip of her tongue along the curve of his lower lip.

'Slow,' he intoned raggedly, and snatched her up to kiss her breathless.

For an endless passage of time it was a battle of wills. Her hands fluttered over every part of him she could reach. She was driven by a deep atavistic need to possess and be possessed, to wipe out days of fevered uncertainty and terrible tension with the passion that made him uniquely hers. She would not be controlled but the jerk of his responsive muscles beneath his smooth bronzed skin, the rawness of his breathing and the thunder of his heart against her exploring fingertips defeated her. His blatant excitement was the most shattering seduction of all.

They came down on the sand in a tangle of limbs, neither one of them able to part for a second. He skimmed off her lace panties with a powerfully impatient hand and she opened her arms to him in an electrifying state of quivering readiness, every inch of her burning and screaming for the fulfillment that only he could give her.

'*Madre di Dio...*' Carlo rasped, coming up for air. 'Did I teach you to do this to me?'

Empowered by a dizzying sense of her own sensuality, Jessica took the opportunity to run her fingers down that intriguing little silky furrow of hair arrowing down over his taut stomach and she found him with shy and shivering pleasure, velvety smooth and hard and...suddenly she was flat on her back, deprived of further journeys of discovery.

She giggled, full of joy and the most wonderful sense of freedom. In retribution, he let his tongue and his teeth rove over her unbearably sensitised breasts and she gritted her teeth and her back arched in agonised response.

'I can't bear it...' she gasped.

'You will,' he assured her.

Her hips began to lift in an expression of need as old as time. He stroked his fingertips over the very heart of her and laughed softly when she moaned, teasing her with the honeyed sweetness of an expert lover, determined to drive her to the outer edge of pleasure before they enjoyed that final union. Time had no meaning. She surrendered to the shuddering instinctive responses that controlled her, lost in the ever-increasing fever of her own excitement.

And when he came to her it was like dying and being reborn in a flash flood of wild sensation. Everything was sharper, hotter and more intense, her body trained to an extraordinary pitch of sensitivity. It was agony and ecstasy, each glorious moment building into an explosive, slow-burning climax that made her sob and gasp in wonder at the peak and then subside, still shivering in the aftermath of an intolerable pleasure.

Carlo smiled down at her, a very male smile of indolent satisfaction. He pressed his lips to her damp cheek and she felt moisture smart behind her eyes. In all her life, she could never recall feeling so outrageously happy.

They washed the sand off in the sea, drank champagne in great thirsty gulps and a little while later made love again. Jessica was more than a little tipsy by the time they strolled down to the jetty and boarded the yacht.

'We'll go sailing all day tomorrow,' Carlo promised.

'And the day after,' she whispered, gripped by this terrible fear that such contentment could not possibly be sustained with other people around.

'If you like.' He led her gently into a cabin, exquisitely furnished with a very large double bed.

She tripped on the edge of a rug and he caught her before she fell. 'I'm drunk on you,' she said, losing herself in the smouldering golden eyes.

'How do you feel about renegotiating our divorce?'

'P-pardon?' She froze.

'As in not having one until we feel the need...*if* we feel the need.' A brilliant smile slashed his gorgeous mouth.

She melted into him with bone-sagging relief. 'I'll think about it,' she said all the same.

The sun was high in the sky when she surfaced from a deep sleep to hear Carlo on the phone.

'What are you doing?'

'Ordering breakfast.'

She was sprawled on top of him, her tousled silver head resting on his chest. It had been the most incredible night. She was adrift on a sea of love so all encompassing it closed out everything else in the world.

'How does being married feel this time?' He ran a caressing finger along one exposed cheekbone and she stretched and tightened her grip on him.

'Good.'

'How to damn with faint praise.'

She smiled voluptuously. 'Fantastic.'

Fast-moving steps sounded somewhere above them. Carlo tensed. Then Marika's voice cried his name.

Carlo sprang out of bed, reached for his jeans and yanked open the door.

Jessica scrambled up but there was no clothing within her grasp. Carlo left the cabin. She heard the swift exchange of Greek, the sob in his sister's shaking voice.

'Lukas has had another attack...' Pale, every facial muscle savagely clenched, Carlo sent Jessica a fleeting, almost blank glance that told her he was already a thousand miles away from her in mind and body.

The honeymoon, she registered, was over.

CHAPTER TEN

JESSICA shivered in spite of the heat. Lukas had left careful instructions for his burial and he had chosen to come back to Greece to the sunbaked hillside where his own parents had been laid to rest. The funeral was small, strictly family but the Press were just beyond the graveyard, a sea of hungry wolves, restrained only by the strong police presence.

'It is time to go.' Marika briefly leant on Jessica's extended arm for support and then straightened again. 'I didn't know I would miss him like this,' she whispered, shaking her greying head. 'But all my life he has been there. For fifty years telling me what to do... I feel lost.'

She wasn't the only one who felt lost. Jessica felt deserted and superfluous to requirements. For days she had told herself not to be childish, not to be selfish, not to expect Carlo to find time for her when his every waking moment was filled with ceaseless demands for his attention. She had innocently expected to make herself useful but had learnt that anything she could do could inevitably be done far more efficiently by a member of his staff. Carlo hadn't just lost a father... Carlo had inherited a vast empire, quaking in the turmoil of Lukas's sudden death.

Carlo had also inherited the devastated and publicly inconsolable widow, Jessica thought grimly. Dear heaven, she *tried* to feel some sense of compassion for Sunny but she had noticed that Sunny invariably wept only in Carlo's vicinity. It was hard to believe that she could be genuinely distressed by her husband's death but if she wasn't, she was certainly putting on a very good show. And there was no doubt that Carlo was impressed by that display. His attitude to Sunny had warmed and softened.

Sunny drooped in unrelieved black beside the grave, a wispy little silk hanky dabbing behind her veil. Carlo hesitated on his way past in a phalanx of male relatives and then paused. Jessica stiffened and looked away, walking ahead with Marika. The cameras went off in a blaze. Jessica flinched.

'Ignore them, Mrs Philippides,' the security man flanking her said. 'You'll soon get used to it.'

But Jessica could not believe that she ever would. From the instant they had left Paradiso Cay she had understood why Lukas had bought an island. At every airport, in every public place, the Press surrounded them in a stifling surge.

'You're hot news,' he sighed as she was slotted into a limousine.

All she wanted to be was hot news to Carlo, who no longer even travelled in the same car with her, it seemed. Nor did he sleep in the same bed very often. He worked through the night, ate at extraordinary hours and never went anywhere with less than three executives tagging on his heels. When she tried to see him, she learnt that she was in the way, and if she hovered and he forgot she was there, she felt humiliated.

'I think I'll go to bed,' Marika mumbled when they reached the opulent house and surrounding estate outside Athens which had once been Lukas's permanent home.

Sunny had made it into Carlo's car. Jessica watched from the window as Sunny was helped out, the very picture of feminine fragility. Jessica's teeth gritted. Maybe I should practise sobbing and throwing hysterics! Childish, you're being childish, the little voice said. She is his father's widow and he takes that tie too seriously to ignore her apparent distress.

Sunny was just an irritation, she told herself in exasperation. A symptom, not the source of the illness. Carlo had married Jessica to please Lukas and now Lukas was dead. She was bitterly aware that the only hold she seemed to have on Carlo was sexual and even that seemed to be on the wane. She had this sinking feeling that their relationship was running fast to its natural conclusion. 'I won't hold you a day after his death,' Carlo had said just days ago. How much strength could she take now from the casual assurance that he wasn't planning on an immediate divorce? Those words had been prompted by the heat of passion on their wedding night.

'Carlo...' She intercepted him in the echoing grandeur of the hall.

'What time do you want to eat?' Sunny talked over her as if she wasn't there.

'Seven.' Hooded dark eyes flicked to Jessica and lingered. 'Hello, stranger,' he said softly.

She moved forward.

'Mr Philippides, the London office is on the line——'

'When would you like this Press release made?'

The twin enquiries from staff stole his attention. He moved on and something simply exploded inside Jessica. 'The next time you want to see me, *you* make an appointment!' she snapped and spun on her heel, stalking back into the drawing-room.

'Bed...by midnight, I promise,' Carlo murmured with soft amusement.

She spun. He had followed her. But they were not truly alone. Just beyond the doorway, his staff awaited them.

'Is it always going to be like this?' she whispered in sudden desperation.

'No, but it will take time to restore calm. Lukas kept a very tight rein on his holdings. He believed in the personal touch. Right to the end he was working an eighteen-hour day,' Carlo drawled wryly. 'He thought he had more time. This is not the smooth transition he envisaged. Everybody's hitting the panic button.'

He should have been exhausted but he wasn't. If anything his aura of vibrant energy was more noticeable. It was beginning to dawn on Jessica that Carlo Saracini no longer existed. This was Lukas Philippides' son, driven, committed and absolutely in his element, she sensed, and the pace was speed up or fall out. Was there a place for her in this new life of his?

Right now, her position felt exceedingly precarious, and that hurt her pride. Jessica bitterly resented the idea that she was slavishly hanging around just waiting for Carlo to take the time and the trouble to reassure her that he *did* want her to stay. And even then, how long did he want her for? Carlo was not in love with her. He had taken his revenge. He had used her to make his father happy. When his hunger for her body faded as it surely would, how could they possibly have any sort of a future together?

She had to dine alone with Sunny. Marika had not emerged from her suite. Faced with Sunny, Jessica wished she had stayed in hers.

'You look terrible,' Sunny sighed, scanning Jessica's shadowed eyes and pallor. 'You should have gone to bed too.'

With a helplessly curled lip, Jessica wondered how the redhead could weep without reddening her eyes. 'I'm not tired,' she said.

'You want me out, don't you?' Sunny guessed. 'But I'm not going anywhere.'

Jessica ignored her.

'You're stuck with me,' Sunny told her with an amused smile. 'I've got nowhere to go. Lukas didn't leave me a bean. I signed a watertight pre-nuptial contract. I'm Carlo's responsibility now.'

Jessica's amethyst eyes flamed. 'And you intend to play it for all you're worth, don't you?'

'Ask Carlo if he wants me to leave,' Sunny suggested softly. 'You see, he doesn't. Carlo likes having me around. He always makes time for me. Haven't you noticed that? It won't be very long before he admits to himself how he really feels about me——'

'I don't want to hear any more of this, Sunny,' Jessica broke in tautly but with dignity.

'But it's the truth. You don't want to see it but Carlo *is* using you. You're the one who's going to be hurt and humiliated,' Sunny asserted confidently. 'Not me. I know the score. I know Carlo——'

'So you keep telling me.'

'He married you to keep Lukas happy, and now Lukas is gone he doesn't need you any more. It's that simple.'

'Carlo is not in love with you,' Jessica told her shortly.

'But he wants me.' Sunny gave her a brilliant smile. 'That's enough, don't you think?'

Jessica rose from the table and walked out of the room. She would not argue with Sunny, thereby lending credibility to her wild claims. For they were wild claims, weren't they? Carlo had yet to betray any sign of *wanting* Sunny. Restively she paced the bedroom floor. She was upset, no point denying that! Sunny was so confident of Carlo... although she hadn't been that night she was drunk, Jessica reminded herself. Then Sunny had said, 'You don't want me... why should you care?' But possibly that had just been a deliberate taunt, a scene engineered to pierce Carlo's tough hide.

Dear heaven, what was she thinking? That it was all true... that Carlo was cold-bloodedly using her? She remembered their wedding-night and could not believe that that had all been pretence. But Jessica reminded herself that Carlo had openly admitted that he had brought her here to keep Sunny at bay. That did not suggest that Carlo was one hundred per cent sure of his ability to withstand the lure of what he already knew was blatantly on offer to him...should he choose to extend a welcoming hand.

She could hardly believe it when Carlo actually made it to bed as he had promised. She sat up, watching him undress with helplessly hungry eyes, but she felt cold inside, resentful that it took the dark of night and his highly sexed nature to bring Carlo to her.

'Is it true that Sunny's staying?' she asked finally because she had to ask, she *had* to know.

The silence stretched; her heartbeat accelerated.

'For the moment, yes,' Carlo murmured.

Jessica took a deep breath. 'Naturally I'm not suggesting you throw her out...but your father owned other houses.'

Carlo sent her a narrowed shrewd glance, his beautifully cut mouth compressing. 'For the moment, she stays here.'

Jessica swallowed hard and then said, 'So you expect me to live with a woman who says she's in love with you and who doesn't seem to give a damn who knows it? Don't you think that's asking a little too much...or is there some special reason why I have to put up with her?'

'*Dio!*' Carlo ground out with sudden savage impatience. 'My father is barely in his grave——'

'Where Sunny wanted him to be.' The interruption leapt recklessly from Jessica's tongue.

Golden eyes blazed over her. 'Like all of us, she says things in distress which she does not mean.'

'She's a damned good actress, I'll give her that!' Jessica snapped back. 'And she's playing you like a fish on a line!'

Pure outrage darkened and hardened Carlo's strong features. 'At this moment, Sunny is my responsibility. She is my father's widow. If I threw her out, where would she go and to whom? I wouldn't do it. She has as much right to be here as you have. She's scared of the future. That is why she is clinging to me.'

'And maybe you enjoy that,' Jessica condemned shakily. 'Macho man and the poor fragile little woman who hangs on his every word. With Sunny beside you, you could turn into a megalomaniac overnight!'

'I'll tell you what I don't enjoy now. Your jealousy,' Carlo returned with blistering derision. 'At least Sunny knows when to shut up and be feminine and warm...'

Jessica went white, lowering her lashes over shocked and wounded eyes. Carlo had turned on her with a biting cruelty unfamiliar to her.

'All I wanted tonight was the sweet oblivion of your body——'

'Sex,' Jessica countered with a shudder of mingled rage and pain.

'Why not? You're my wife,' Carlo slung back at her harshly.

Dear God, was that all their marriage meant to him? Was she just an available body? Or was she merely a temporary substitute for Sunny until such time as he deemed it acceptable for him to bed his father's widow? Jessica was devastated by the suspicion but when Carlo compared her unfavourably to Sunny suspicion found foundation in fact. It was not as though Carlo loved his wife, not as though they had married for any of the more usual reasons... She was in agony.

'I don't want you,' she mumbled.

'Then you won't object if I find someone who does, will you?' Carlo delivered with cut-glass precision but he slammed the door so hard that she wouldn't have been surprised if it fell off its hinges.

He doesn't mean it... he's being dramatic... he can't stand it when you say you don't want him, she told herself. Then she burst into tears but that made her feel worse. She propped her chin on her hand and reflected for a long time. Where were her wits? Why had she thrown a scene like that?

Carlo might not be showing it but he was under immense strain. He hadn't even had twelve hours' breathing space to grieve for Lukas and he had been flung in at the deep end of his father's vast business empire and forced to take charge. She shouldn't have attacked him about Sunny. He had wanted warmth and why not? Right now, the bedroom was the only place they were alone, the only place he could relax, and she had driven him away!

Sunny didn't give up the chase easily. She knew Carlo was not in love with his wife and that encouraged her. She was just trying to cause trouble by playing on Jessica's insecurity and Carlo's infuriating sense of what was due to his father's widow. What a fool she would be to allow a bimbo like Sunny to come between her and Carlo!

Jessica slid out of bed and pulled on a lacy peignoir. He had said that she didn't trust him, that she didn't have faith, and she was about to prove him wrong for a change. When life was calmer, she would tell him what she was having to take from Sunny and then he might understand just how offensive she found the situation. She was a big girl, wasn't she? She could deal with Sunny herself.

The house was silent but the corridors fully lit. Wryly, it occurred to her that she couldn't go barging into all the bedrooms in search of Carlo. But maybe he hadn't gone to bed yet. As she descended the main staircase, she saw a dim light showing below the library door and thought, Bingo!

Only she didn't hit the jackpot she expected when she quietly turned the handle and opened the door, intending to surprise him. Every muscle in her slender body jerked painfully tight. There was a roaring in her eardrums and for a split-second she thought she was going to pass out.

Carlo was sprawled along a comfortable sofa with Sunny in his arms. Both of them were fast asleep in the indolent, relaxed positions of lovers, Sunny's wonderful hair trailing like a banner across his chest, one of her hands resting loosely on his shoulder.

Later, she didn't recall actually stepping back and closing the door again, but she did recall her absolute terror of them waking up and seeing her standing there, gaping at them. She mounted the stairs again, returned to their bedroom and lifted the phone.

'I want a car to the airport now. Mr Philippides is asleep. There's no need to disturb him.' An hysterical laugh nearly choked her at that point. She reckoned that it would have taken an avalanche to disturb either of them. Lying there totally at peace on the same day as the very funeral. Dear God, how could he?

He had to *want* her, just as she had said. Maybe they hadn't even made love yet...Carlo had still been clothed, Sunny in one of her drapy white silk nightgowns. Did it matter? They had looked like bloody Romeo and Juliet, she thought sickly, so torn apart by what she had seen, she was still shaking all over with shock.

'So what *can* I tell him?' Gerald Amory enquired thinly.

'Nothing.' Jessica kept on sipping at her cup of coffee, holding it like a barrier in front of her drawn face.

'All right,' her father spelt out flatly. 'I can accept that you made a mistake rushing into marriage with him, but at least you could have the gumption to tell him that to his face instead of running away and hiding!'

She chewed nervously at her lower lip. It hurt that her father should be on Carlo's side. But how did she tell her father the truth? If she did, he would probably feel he couldn't work for Carlo any more, and he might throw up his new job and then where would he be?

'Are you pregnant?'

Jessica stared in astonishment.

Gerald sighed. 'Carlo thought you might be ... hormones putting you round the twist or some such thing.'

'I am not pregnant or crazy, thank you very much!'

'Well, you look awful. You've lost a lot of weight.'

Silence fell, uneasy, tense.

'Every time he phones me, I feel worse,' her father persisted. 'He knows that we're in contact with each other. He knows that I know where you are.'

If she had had the energy left, she would have hated Carlo for putting her in such a position. What on earth was he playing at? In the six weeks since she had left Greece, it had become painfully obvious that Carlo had no intention of going public with his relationship with his former stepmother. Maybe he thought it was too soon, or maybe Carlo was quite happy just to have Sunny in his bed in secret.

Having run the gamut of every possible conjecture, Jessica had learnt that ultimately it really didn't matter. Carlo wanted Sunny. Sheer uncontrollable lust, or love— what difference did it make? Jessica just wanted to be left alone with the most intolerable burden of misery she had ever endured.

'He's worried sick about you.'

'Breaking his heart, no doubt,' Jessica muttered tightly.

'Why can't you see him?'

Because pride was all she had left, and if she saw him she might let herself down badly. Carlo didn't know that she had fallen in love with him and she didn't want him to know.

Her father took his leave, close-mouthed and disapproving. Having come down to London on business, he was flying back to Glasgow where he had recently embarked on his new job. Jessica looked round her tiny flatlet, over-furnished with her possessions from the cottage. She hadn't been able to find a permanent secretarial position yet. She had signed up with a temping agency and with the aid of some savings was just about managing to survive. But one day blurred with terrifying blankness into the next.

It was around ten when someone knocked on the door. She was on her way to bed and grimaced. Her nextdoor neighbour, a rather pushy male in his late twenties, had been putting his all into trying to chat her up this week, calling round at odd times, refusing to take no for an answer...

Exasperated, she opened the door and then fell back a step, the colour draining from her cheeks, shock currenting through her in debilitating waves. Carlo dealt her a razor-edged smile from the vantage point of his greatly superior height and thrust the door shut behind him with a powerful hand.

'Your father was followed. I knew he would meet up with you sooner or later,' Carlo imparted grimly.

'You had no right to do that!'

But she couldn't take her eyes off him. In a superbly cut pearl-grey suit that sleekly outlined his lean, muscular physique, a white silk shirt highlighting the gold of his skin and the darkness of his hair, Carlo looked breathtakingly handsome. His impact slivered through her nerve-endings, leaving her disturbingly aware of his every movement and badly shaken. She felt horribly like a plant left to wither forgotten on a windowsill suddenly being tantalised with a jug of life-giving water.

'You are going to crawl by the time I'm finished with you,' Carlo sizzled down at her, emanating temper and arrogance and self-satisfaction in perceptible waves.

'I don't think so.' Squaring her slight shoulders, Jessica slung him a look of pure scorn, denying the craving that he could evoke inside her even when he was demonstrating all in one go all the less pleasant characteristics of his powerful personality.

'You have a VCR?' Seeing it for himself, Carlo headed for it in one long stride and deposited two videotapes beside it. 'We'll probably still be sitting here at lunchtime tomorrow. You are going to watch and inwardly digest every unutterably boring hour of this just as I had to——'

'Carlo...w-what are you talking about?' she prompted, watching him feed in a tape with incredulous eyes.

'It was several weeks before it occurred to me that you might have taken off for a reason ... as opposed to being just sheer bloody contrary!' he raked at her, suddenly sizzling with rage. 'And I was furious with you. I couldn't wait to get my hands on you. Then I dug out these tapes and I wanted to strangle you!'

The tip of her tongue snaked out to dry her lips. What the blazes was he rattling on about? What were those tapes? The TV screen came alive with a most disorientating overhead view of the library outside Athens. It was eerie. Jessica gaped, totally dazed by the sight of Carlo striding through the door, pouring himself a large drink and then throwing himself on that self-same sofa.

'Every reception-room and every corridor in my father's houses are protected by twenty-four-hour sur-

veillance equipment. Only the bedrooms and the bathrooms are off limits,' Carlo informed her. 'You can see
the date and the exact time displayed at the foot of the
picture.'

'Yes,' she quavered.

'And now you can watch me fall asleep...really riv-
eting stuff. Sunny makes her entrance in about half an
hour——'

'Sunny,' she echoed weakly.

'I could have had the tapes cut to speed this up but I
didn't want to spare you a single second of the
entertainment.'

Swallowing hard, Jessica dutifully watched Carlo
falling asleep, the most awful suspicion beginning to
assail her. 'You can fast forward if you like,' she
mumbled in a small voice.

'Are you sure?'

'Quite sure.'

With a sinking heart, Jessica watched Sunny creep in
and stand gazing down at Carlo. A little while later, she
curled up beside him and put her arms round him. A
long while after that, Carlo shifted in his sleep and curved
an arm round Sunny.

'I don't want to see any more,' Jessica told him, unable
to meet his eyes.

'I insist,' Carlo said harshly. 'The sole highlight is entry
of the betrayed wife.'

Her legs wouldn't hold her up any longer. She collapsed down on to the settee.

'We're on to the second tape before I wake up and
chuck her out.'

'I don't need to watch it.'

He didn't switch it off. Through her straining fingers,
Jessica caught a glimpse of her own entrance and it
looked almost comic on camera, only the memory of
how she had felt still cut into her painfully. Carlo had

simply fallen asleep and Sunny had wrapped herself round him.

'I was exhausted that night. I slept like the dead.' Carlo uttered a sardonic laugh, his dark features tautening.

'How could I know that it was innocent?' Jessica whispered. 'I thought that you wanted her. She was so sure that you did——'

'My father's leavings?' Carlo breathed with distaste.

Jessica lifted her silvery head in disbelief. His revulsion at the idea was unconcealed. 'But...but you said she was stunningly eye-catching——'

'So she is, but I have never found her sexually attractive. She reminded me of Bella. Vain, self-centred, thick as a brick apart from a certain greedy streak of native cunning when it comes to feathering her own nest——'

'Thick as a brick?' Jessica echoed, licking her dry lips in shock.

'Enjoy many scintillating conversations with her, did you?'

'Well...no, but you seemed so keen to keep her around; I thought——'

'You really expected me to chuck her out the day of the funeral?' Carlo enquired gently.

Jessica reddened. 'You should have told me how you felt about her.'

'I thought it was obvious...and you didn't ask,' Carlo reminded her drily. 'Until we had that stupid argument, I had no idea she even bothered you. You came at me out of the blue and I was in a bad mood.' Unusually, he hesitated, his sensual mouth twisting. 'I don't pay much attention to Sunny, I have to admit. I did think she'd given up on her aspiration to move from my father's bed to mine——'

'Like hell she had,' Jessica muttered feelingly.

'So I discovered. That night I woke up to find her wrapped round me like a boa constrictor, I was disgusted with her. I knew she wasn't in love with me. The first time Sunny looked at herself in a mirror she fell in love for the rest of her life,' Carlo drawled with an expressive grimace. 'I paid her off. The minute she got that cheque in her hand, she was off like a hare for pastures new. She won't approach me again. She hates me like poison now. I don't think it had ever crossed Sunny's mind that a man *could* find her repulsive.'

That was music to Jessica's ears. Carlo had fulfilled what he felt to be his obligations to his former stepmother and if Jessica had only given him time, he would have done that while they were still living together. She knew then that she had to tell him what she had been forced to tolerate from Sunny.

His state of shock by the time she had finished speaking spoke for him. He had had no suspicion that Sunny was putting that much effort into undermining their relationship.

A disturbing silence fell then. Jessica began to wonder if Carlo had gone to all this trouble to force her to face him merely to prove that he had not been guilty of lusting after Sunny.

'I've also been thinking,' Carlo finally said heavily, 'about how much I allowed what happened with Bella to influence my attitude to you. Six years ago, I suspect you paid some of her dues for her. I was still pretty bitter. My ego was still smarting. I was determined that the next woman I wanted would come to me only on my terms. I didn't trust my own emotions. I wouldn't admit how strong my feelings for you were.'

'Strong?' Disturbed by the gravity of his mood, Jessica prompted him uncertainly.

'I was in love with you,' Carlo confessed harshly, and it was as if the admission had been tortured out of him.

'In love with me?' she whispered dazedly, and she couldn't even get excited by the revelation when he looked so grim about giving her that knowledge. She collided with shimmering golden eyes and sensed that for the very first time she was hearing the truth, not parts of it but *all* of it.

'Did you never ask yourself why I behaved as I did? Do you really believe I would have gone to so much trouble merely to get you into bed?' Carlo prompted with a derisive twist to his strained mouth. 'It was my misfortune to fall for a woman on the brink of marrying another man. I wanted time with you and you wouldn't give me that time...and what was worst of all was knowing that you were fighting an attraction as strong as mine right from the beginning!'

'Yes,' she acknowledged unsteadily. 'But I didn't recognise that attraction for what it was. I was terrified of it.' She flushed unhappily and tried to laugh. 'I thought I was turning into a scarlet woman, but——'

'You hurt me as Bella never had the power to hurt me,' Carlo cut in flatly.

Hot moisture stung her eyes. She saw the truth of that statement in his expressive eyes. That was another first. He wasn't shielding his emotions from her. His guard was down.

'When I was informed that your father had been helping himself to company funds,' Carlo continued levelly, 'I was delighted. In fact, I was triumphant...'

'Yes,' she said painfully. 'I knew that.'

'And you were right, I didn't give a damn about Gerald. All I saw was a very useful weapon. I could have handled Sunny on my own if I'd needed to,' Carlo drawled half under his breath. 'What I really wanted more than anything was to get you flat on your back on the nearest bed and make you pay for walking out on me six years ago——'

'You wanted revenge. I kn-knew that,' she asserted
shakily, moving away from him, no longer able to bear
any form of proximity. It was over, wasn't that what he
was telling her? He had dealt with Sunny; now it was
her turn.

Carlo drove not quite steady fingers through his thick
black hair, looking less in command of himself than was
the norm. 'I'd be lying if I said I regretted it. I didn't...I
don't,' he adjusted, seemingly bent on giving her the
kind of honesty that only hurt her more. 'I didn't care
what methods I had to use to get you back——'

'Tell me something I don't know!' Jessica condemned
in a choked voice, desperately fighting off tears of pain
and an increasing urge to show him the door.

There was a long silence and then, Carlo expelled his
breath sharply. 'I still love you...'

There was an even longer silence while she stared back
at him in shock, afraid to trust her own hearing.

'Still?' It was a whisper of awed hope. 'You still love
me?'

'What the hell do you think I'm doing here with those
tapes?' he demanded roughly.

'You were pretty objectionable when you came
through the door——'

'You walked out on me——'

'And you thought of the last time.' With a look of
remorse, she flung herself into his arms. 'Carlo...don't
you know when you've won?'

He trembled against her. 'Won?' he repeated
uncertainly.

'Don't you know that I love you?'

With a groan, he crushed her into a fevered embrace.
'We've been stalking each other like wary animals!' he
vented furiously. 'How long have you loved me?'

'It feels like forever,' she mumbled truthfully. 'As if I woke up one day when I was twenty and there you were and I've never been free of you since——'

He muttered a driven imprecation, deciding that they were both talking too much, and swept her off her feet.

'The bed's through there,' she murmured helpfully.

His slashing sensual smile plunged her into an ecstasy of anticipation.

'Want me?' he breathed, standing over her, removing his clothes with far more haste than cool.

'Desperately.'

'No divorce.'

'Absolutely not.'

'Children?'

As he came down beside her, she laughed for pure joy. 'What is this?'

'The blueprint for the rest of our lives.' Rolling over, he pinned her beneath him, glittering golden eyes clinging to her delighted face. 'I am crazy about you——'

'I wish you had told me instead of my father!'

'I wanted you to say it first...how could you think I wanted a woman like Sunny?' he abruptly demanded.

'She kept on telling me you did.'

'And what about what I was telling you on our wedding-night?'

As he ran a possessive hand up to one pouting breast, she shivered deliciously and struggled to concentrate but really it was very difficult. 'We didn't get enough time together...I suppose I'll have to get used to that——'

'No. I don't want to live as Lukas did. I'm selling up...consolidating...delegating,' he enumerated raggedly, following every newly discovered curve of female flesh with positively compulsive intensity. 'Anything I can do within reason to avoid working a seven-day week. Unlike my father, I've been fortunate enough to find happiness with one woman and I don't intend to lose it again.'

'You couldn't lose me,' Jessica sighed ecstatically under the scorching heat of his hungry hands.

'I very nearly did,' Carlo breathed harshly. 'I should have told you I loved you.'

'I love you,' she said soothingly.

'I think we need a long vacation,' Carlo sighed, a very long time later after they had made love.

'No phone,' she said.

'An answering machine?' he bargained.

'And possibly...' Amethyst eyes rested on him hopefully. 'A lift?'

His darkly handsome features slashed with vibrant amusement. 'Definitely...a lift,' he agreed.

Breathtaking romance is predicted in your future with Harlequin's newest collection: Fortune Cookie.

Three of your favorite Harlequin authors, Janice Kaiser, Margaret St. George and M.J. Rodgers will regale you with the romantic adventures of three heroines who are promised fame, fortune, danger and intrigue when they crack open their fortune cookies on a fateful night at a Chinese restaurant.

Join in the adventure with your own personalized fortune, inserted in every book!

Don't miss this exciting new collection!

Available in September
wherever Harlequin books are sold.

HARLEQUIN®

HARLEQUIN WOMEN KNOW ROMANCE WHEN THEY SEE IT.

And they'll see it on **ROMANCE CLASSICS**, the new 24-hour TV channel devoted to romantic movies and original programs like the special **Harlequin** Showcase of Authors & Stories.

The **Harlequin** Showcase of Authors & Stories introduces you to many of your favorite romance authors in a program developed exclusively for Harlequin readers.

Watch for the **Harlequin** Showcase of **Authors & Stories** series beginning in the summer of 1997.

If you're not receiving ROMANCE CLASSICS, call your local cable operator or satellite provider and ask for it today!

Escape to the network of your dreams.

ROMANCE CLASSICS

HARLEQUIN 🜔 PRESENTS®

Coming in September...

Breaking Making Up

by
Miranda Lee and
Susan Napier

Two original stories in one unique volume—
"Two for the price of one!"

Meet two irresistible men from
Down Under— one Aussie, one Kiwi.
The time has come for them to settle old scores
and win the women they've always wanted!

Look for Breaking Making Up (#1907)
in September 1997.

Available wherever Harlequin books are sold.

**HARLEQUIN AND SILHOUETTE
ARE PLEASED TO PRESENT**

Born in the USA

Love, marriage—and the pursuit of family!

Check your retail shelves for these upcoming titles:

July 1997
Last Chance Cafe by Curtiss Ann Matlock
The most determined bachelor in Oklahoma is in trouble! A
lovely widow with three daughters has moved next door—and
the girls want a dad! But he wants to know if their mom needs
a husband....

August 1997
Thorne's Wife by Joan Hohl
Pennsylvania. It was only to be a marriage of convenience—
until they fell in love! Now, three years later, tragedy
threatens to separate them forever and Valerie wants only to
be in the strength of her husband's arms. For she has some
very special news for the expectant father...

September 1997
Desperate Measures by Paula Detmer Riggs
New Mexico judge Amanda Wainwright's daughter has been
kidnapped, and the price of her freedom is a verdict in
favor of a notorious crime boss. So enters ex-FBI agent
Devlin Buchanan—ruthless, unstoppable—and soon there is
no risk he will not take for her.

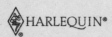 
HARLEQUIN®   Silhouette®

BUSA2